The Story of

THE SARASOTA
ASSASSINATION SOCIETY

A Novel

The Story of

THE SARASOTA
ASSASSINATION SOCIETY

TONY DUNBAR

Blind Pass Publications
Florida

Early settlors Carrie Abbe, whose father, Postmaster Charles E. Abbe was murdered by the Vigilantes, and her husband Anton Kleinoscheg. Courtesy Jeff LaHurd.

Blind Pass Publications, LLC
Post Office Box 1096
Englewood, FL 34223

PROMISE

This story is about fifty percent true.

DEDICATION

Naething could resist my Nancy

– Robert Burns

THE SARASOTA
ASSASSINATION SOCIETY

A NOVEL

I was a cocky little bastard back then. I say this with the benefit of hindsight. My, how the decades do pass. I can now attest that my 18-year-old self was ready and randy and not too smart. Certainly not worldly, having spent my youth on an orange farm, bunking in a barn, taking my meals with the Ephrams, the black family that worked the place for Sandy Watson, who was the County Sheriff. I had cows and horses for company. And all the wildlife you can imagine roaming Southwest Florida, which in those faraway days was a frontier wilderness. And I had Reuben, a few years older than I was, who was the adopted gift of the Ephrams, who had three children of their own.

Too young by today's conventions, I embarked on a manhunt and single-handedly brought in a cold-blooded murderer. That experience determined who, what and where I am today, unimportant as that may be to the world at large. But looking back, it's hard not to be proud of that green 18-year-old. And now that I have time to reflect on that and other passages in my life, I will try to put some of it down, all the way back to about 1884.

Some of the story I will relate as it was told to me. Some I'll have to imagine, based on what I heard and saw. But for the most part, I was there.

My name is Gawain Wallace MacFarlane, and I'm now an almost famous lawman.

TABLE OF CONTENTS

CHAPTER ONE

FLORIDA STORIES

A very strange private men's club assembled in a gloomy room, lit only by the glow of moonlight through a dirty window. One of the attendees closed the shutters and struck a match to an oil lantern hanging from the rafters.

The six shadowy figures were gathered around a stove situated in the middle of the store. As usual there wasn't a fire in it since winter nights in Florida generally didn't call for one, but sitting around the stove was just the natural place to discuss weighty matters like the one at hand, which was murder. These were evil men.

As the flame in the lantern got brighter, it illuminated shelves neatly stacked with sacks of dried beans and canned goods. A colorful campaign poster for Grover Cleveland and Thomas Hendricks, the "Hoosier Irishman," was tacked to the wall above a brass National Cash Register, the most impressive fixture in the room.

All of the men knew each other since they were a sizeable portion of the total population of their emerging fishing village, Sara Sota, or as it was coming to be called, Sarasota. The village was a small and scattered collection of houses, some competently made and carefully erected with milled and dried lumber, while others were just colorful tropical shanties, all separated from each other by palm trees and vegetable gardens. The hamlet did boast two general stores, the present meeting being held in Bidwell's. Both stores sold all manner of groceries and hardware, from foot powder to mule harnesses. In anticipation of tourists, jars of orange blossom honey and bins of seashells were stacked by the door.

In Sarasota's "downtown," centered around the two stores, the few shops and buildings were arrayed on sandy walkways or lanes only wide enough for a wagon to pass, all oriented to the bay. At waterside, small docks received the mail boat and, hopefully, visitors. The docks were also used to offload fish, dry the catch and send it away by schooner to be sold as far north as Tampa and as far south as Key West. Inland, there was some experimental orange and grapefruit production, but the primary occupations of the townsfolk all revolved around the water: boat building, commerce by sail up and down the coast, and always the endless bounty of fish, mullet primarily, which multiplied plentifully in the sparkling bay and the Gulf of Mexico.

Nets needing mending were draped on wood frames all along the beaches. A few new houses were starting to go up as more Yankees discovered the area and moved in. Prospects were good that a real hotel would be built one day soon; boosters of it suggested that it would offer one hundred rooms. And, a good hotel could attract wealthy visitors who wanted to experience "America's Tropics" by catching tarpon, flipping turtles, shooting alligators, and those seeking relief from a whole assortment of debilitating illnesses that would be cured or certainly bettered by endless sunshine.

But I'm wandering away from my story. This meeting of the men's club was a secret gathering. Two of those whispering around the stovepipe were dressed for toil and naturally scruffy. They were Joe Anderson and Ed Bacon, who both tonged for oysters and farmed a bit. Lounging between them was a young man, Charley Willard, who seemed tall even when seated. His clothes weren't particularly clean, but he had a neatly trimmed mustache and considered himself a charmer with the ladies. Most people liked him, at least when he was sober. Then there were two "doctors," though only one of them actually practiced medicine. Dr. Adam Hunter, a small gray-haired man of 40 or 50, was a clerk in Bidwell's store. He rubbed his hands together to help himself think. Dr. Leonard Andrews, the real doctor, was tall and severe and dressed in shirtsleeves and a tie. He had a very red face and gray hair streaked with white. The doctor's scientific skills were rudimentary but satisfactory by local standards, and he was active in his church. He also farmed ten acres on Bee Ridge where he produced oranges, eggs and honey. He was originally from Iowa.

The sixth, Alfred Bidwell, owned the place. He was middle-aged and partly bald. He had coarse but tidy chin whiskers, and he wore a starched shirt covered by a loose black jacket. Time would prove him to be the most devious of the lot, and he was doing most of the talking. A bottle passed slowly from hand to hand. When it came to Bidwell, he shook his head, though he was the one who had produced it from a shelf under the counter. The product was a local corn whiskey, not Bidwell's bracer of choice.

A seventh man had been pacing nervously on the porch outside. He was Lewis Cato, a bootlegger and farmer with rough calloused hands. Bidwell sent his clerk, Hunter, to blindfold Cato and escort him in. The novitiate was brought into the circle and Bidwell had him kneel. Then he stripped off the blindfold, held up his right hand, and gave him the oath of secrecy on pain of death. "It was the tightest oath I ever swallowed," Cato said afterwards. "We were supposed to do, or die." He was given a chair with the rest.

Bidwell resumed the floor. "As all of you know, the way our society works is, you're either in it or out," he said solemnly. He had the trace of a lisp which he artfully concealed by avoiding certain words. "And all of you are in, if you don't run out the door right now." Whatever apprehension they may have felt, no one got up and ran.

"That's the way it's going to be then," Bidwell said. "You are all leaders in the Sarasota Vigilance Society. Fellows, there is no going back!" He looked around, collecting nods. "The purpose of the society is to clean house in our community," he continued. "Each of you knows who I'm talking about, and anyone who can't take orders and don't do what needs to be done, well they've got to be taken care of on the spot."

"Are we supposed to wear robes and burn crosses?" Joe Anderson asked nervously. "I don't go for that queer stuff."

"No," Bidwell assured him. "None of that. We're not out to scare people, though there's some that a good thrashing would improve. Our business is more serious than that. A number of our neighbors, you know who they are, have got to be put out of the way permanently. I repeat, permanently! Now does everybody understand? Well, you'd better. You know too much now to say 'no'."

"It don't seem like there's very many of us," one of the men pointed out.

"Don't you worry about that," Bidwell assured him. "There's plenty more in our organization and plenty more that want to join. More than twenty leading men from all around Manatee County are already with us. And we'll get damn near every Democrat hereabouts involved in due course. We'll clean out the privy and set things right, if we all stick together. If any man doesn't want to join in, he can go to hell!"

This was certainly the best speech of Bidwell's vigilante career.

ALFRED BIDWELL'S STORY

My brother Dan was always the golden child in our family and carried on our long and honorable tradition of military service. Not just that. He managed our family's firm, building ships to sail the Great lakes. I was never more than the bookkeeper. It was Dan who had the name in the community, who was popular enough to be appointed Justice of the Peace

5

and who got himself elected Police Juror in our section of Buffalo, New York.

When South Carolina seceded, Dan was the first to volunteer for the Union and follow our old man's footsteps. Father had fought a guerilla war against the British in the War of 1812, and my young mother, clutching Dan to her bosom, was driven from her home by advancing red-coats and ran through the woods while their cannon balls crashed through the trees around her. I heard this story over and over. Dan was baby number one. I was number eight.

Once the Civil War started, Dan was made a Colonel by his men's acclaim, then a General, then a hero, shot dead from the saddle at Spotsylvania. For him they make speeches and erect statues. Only Dan is mentioned in my mother's memoirs.

My fate was to run a general merchandise shop with my unhappy wife in our freezing-cold city. As chance would have it my wife disappeared – ran off to California they said – and her sudden departure left me free to marry, without undue ceremony, a lady with substantial assets. We had heard about Florida, and decided to make our new life there.

Florida was the last frontier and Sarasota was a town where a smart man could succeed, could open a community store, and prosper mightily. The little village, ready to boom, needed someone to build the finest house, to assert political will, and to know everyone's business. The only trouble was there was somebody else already doing that, Mister Charles Abbe, and he had gotten here ten years before me.

Abbe already ran a grocery and hardware store, very similar to the one I started. He had a nice house, and he was a big-shot Yankee who had arrived in the community right after the War ended. The Reconstruction years cleared the way for him to scoop up hundreds of prime acres on the Bay. He naturally grabbed the job of town Postmaster, since he was the town Republican. He reminded me a lot of my late brother, taking advantage of every situation. But, unlike my brother, he wasn't so universally popular.

My new wife purchased a big lot on a bluff near the water, and we started to build our home. And she bought an old boat-house on the Bay. It was to be my general store. I was right across Hudson's Bayou from Abbe's, my main competitor.

My customers were common people, people not impressed by a Yankee so-called progressive. They overlooked the fact that I was New York-raised, and, fortunately, they had never heard of the dead Yankee hero, General Daniel D. Bidwell.

A man named Jason Alford became my neighbor in 1882, after his home place burned down out in the Bee Ridge settlement. His young wife owned a little cottage right behind my store. They were from Georgia originally. Jason and I took a liking to each other and shared political sentiments. Alford brought in the Bee Ridge trade. That's how I met Joe Anderson, who had also moved into town from Bee Ridge, and Dr. Leonard Andrews, who still lived out in the country where he had a good medical practice.

We all shared the same discontents and hopes. Here on Sara Sota Bay, all of the best land was in Postmaster Abbe's hands, but the major interests were opposed to him. Go a bit inland and you'd see miles of vacant land settled sparsely by people who owned only as much as they could protect. A lot of what you saw was land the State of Florida sold to a Philadelphia lawyer named Disston. It was a squalid deal advertised as a public good but it greatly profited the corrupt politicians in Tallahassee. Yet it opened up competing title claims, bigger and bigger real estate transactions, and opportunities for a small dedicated group to take control of the law and the local morals and make money.

   In December of 1884, a family of Barlows, squatters I suppose, lived in a cabin they had put together from logs and rough pine planks that had been discarded by a sawmill, sheltered under a roof of tin sheets salvaged from a burned down church. They were somewhere east of the Myakka River and west of the Peace River, near the Buzzard Roost Branch of Horse Creek, no man's land. Or, you might say, no man's but theirs.

They been driven to this spot from South Georgia, where "Pa" Barlow had gotten mixed up in some social unrest and agitation involving severe wage cuts for turpentine tappers, of which he was one. He came close to getting shot by the company's hired killers during the worst of the dispute, and he had barely time enough to grab his wife and daughter and make a run for it. Together they fled to Southwest Florida, a land even more remote from civilization than the unimaginably hot piney backwoods of Georgia.

Pa Barlow worked a little here and there on the wandering path south, trying to keep his family fed. His wife, Lovelady, cooked, did cleaning for ladies when she could, and cared for their daughter. They slept in a tent made out of blankets in the forest at the edges of countless settlements with names that have long since been forgotten.

"Pa" and Lovelady quit desiring to have another baby, and stopped making love, and even stopped grumbling about the poor food, the rough road, and the unfriendly and suspicious people they encountered all along the way. They got used to the silence between them. "Pa" had been more respectable once and had even been a sawmill foreman in Georgia, but the depression of '82 knocked him back to being a common laborer. Lovelady had been raised even higher up in society. Her dad was a Georgia peach grower and owned his own farm, but, as a girl-too-young, she had run away to be with "Pa," whose given name was really Nasby.

The fruit of their union, a daughter they named Clarinda, never got to go to school except for a few months when they were living down the road from a lumber camp. The girl grew up accustomed to working hard, riding horses, and, once they were vagabonds, eating stolen chickens, smokehouse pork and fruit scavenged from the public whose homes they camped near. Lovelady looked after the youngster as best she could, but, like their spirits, the family's clothes were worn to tatters and their faces were etched by the constant strain of their difficult circumstances.

The Barlows ran out of road somewhere south of "old Myakka Village" by the headwaters of the river of that name, and just kept on going, with a wagon, one horse, and one "borrowed" cow, until they ran out of people as well. On some high ground in a hardwood hammock, Pa decided it was time to make their stand and build a house, thatched and sided with palm fronds. At first there was only wild game to eat, when they could catch it with a net or a trap. For vegetables they had poke weed and cabbage palm stew. Time passed and things gradually got better, but not that much.

 The Barlow homestead grew from a tarpaulin stretched over

sticks to a solid pine cabin chinked with clay, then it was extended with a kitchen. The three family members built a crude coral and a lean-to for a stable, and their garden started to grow.

Clarinda grew, too, and became more aware of the inner life of her parents. They argued a lot. She sometimes watched her mother stare into the handheld mirror Lovelady had always treasured, pressing her fingertips against the lines around her eyes and under her chin, pushing her forehead up to her hair, trying to smooth out her skin, once so delicate. The face staring back at her was sad, but determined. Determined for what? the girl wondered, hearing her mother say "Damn" under her breath as she studied her reflection. Clarinda got to be sixteen years old.

Her mother took note of the birthday, and made Clarinda a dress out of a bolt of white linen. She stitched intricate depictions of grapes and peaches on it. When the dress was finished Clarinda tried it on. Until then she had always worn handmade dungarees and a flannel shirt. Lovelady saw the surprise and joy radiating from her daughter's face and broke down crying.

"Mama, what's wrong?" Clarinda asked. "It's a beautiful dress. The prettiest thing I ever saw."

"Nothing, honey. I just wish it could be something more." Lovelady mopped her eyes with a dishtowel. "I'm just not doing very good these days."

"Things ain't too bad, mama. We got potatoes coming up. There's still corn in the back."

"That's right, my baby. It's just me. It's just I always told you to try to be kind to folks."

"I do."

"And I know that. The thing is, honey, I'm forgetting how to be kind."

They both stepped back from the conversation and got supper on the table. Lovelady put the dress away in a chest, for some special occasion, she told her daughter.

The next morning, Lovelady was gone. She didn't take the horse; how she got away they never knew. Pa spent an hour thrashing about in the woods, thinking maybe a bear got her. But she had left Clarinda's dress laid out on the kitchen table with little red flowers arranged on it in the shape of a heart. So it didn't look like they could blame any bear.

CHAPTER TWO

DARK DAYS

Now we get back to things I know more about. Sarasota used to be a rough place to live in. On Saturday nights, lured by moonshine and smuggled Cuban rum, cowboys came in from the scrub prairies where they had spent the week capturing and branding wild cattle. They called themselves crackers but were quick to take offense when addressed that way by anybody else. They would ride down the sandy roads past the remote log and pine-planked houses, firing pistols through the palm trees at the moon. And what a moon! Nothing was more beautiful and haunting than the huge moon lighting the waves running through the big pass into Sarasota Bay from the Gulf of Mexico.

Murderers in our vicinity rarely made it to the courthouse for their punishment. The locals took it into their own hands to see justice done, usually at the end of a rope. In spite of the general lawlessness of the place, its citizens were quite litigious when it came to suing each other. They seemed enamored with the legal system that came in with progress, and they used it relentlessly to agitate their neighbors.

One of the victims of the litigious fever was the small community's Postmaster, Charles Abbe. The post office was situated in his general store. Abbe somehow stirred up the enmity of certain of the townsfolk, causing them to bring a barrage of spurious charges and lawsuits against him. The basis of the friction was hard to pin-point. He was somewhat of a newcomer – of more than ten years – but most of his adversaries had lived there less than that. He was relatively wealthy – money made selling Singer Sewing Machines in the Midwest, and he had gotten to town early enough and with enough cash or credit to buy some prime real estate where the town would grow. He also enjoyed the benefits of Republican patronage, and, in addition to being postmaster, he was appointed U.S. Land Commissioner to adjudicate property disputes for the federal district court. The district encompassed thousands of square miles, so Abbe had a lot of sway. As U.S. Land Commissioner, he was known for giving squatters defending their land claims their day in court, which might have been the real source of his problems since wealthy developer types had little use for the rights of poor squatters.

The charges brought against the postmaster were frivolous. One of his accusers was Jason Alford, grocer Bidwell's Georgian friend and neighbor. He had Abbe charged with selling whiskey illegally, for 25 cents a pint at the general store. Alford said he knew this knew this first-hand because he had bought the bootleg product and enjoyed it despite the disagreement about the price. Additional trifling charges included selling quinine without a license and running a boarding house.

None of the complaints against the postmaster went anywhere, but they still required him to make numerous trips to the Manatee County courthouse at Pine Level, an outpost far away from everywhere. The location of the courthouse had been selected by victorious Unionists at War's end who thought the remote location might disrupt the pleasant lives of the old Confederate courthouse gang which was entrenched on both banks of the Manatee River near its mouth at the north end of the county. The Pine Level courthouse was forty miles away from there and more than a day's travel for everybody else except for the saloon keepers and country lawyers who settled in close proximity.

When their legal charges against Abbe failed, several good citizens launched an outlaw crusade against the postmaster. Someone girdled the prized orange trees he used to demonstrate new and potentially enriching agricultural techniques - some of which he had picked up from the innovative Reasoner brothers from Princeton, Illinois, who had settled nearby. While Abbe was travelling up North to peddle his citrus groves and real estate to potential pioneers, a person, suspected to be the esteemed Dr. Leonard Andrews, fired a gun outside Abbe's home on a night while the absent postmaster's wife was inside, frightening her near to death.

DR. LEONARD ANDREWS' STORY

I grew up in Cass County, Iowa, on Turkey Creek right beside the road the Mormon's took. In my part of Iowa we were no strangers to vigilantes. Secret societies and oaths, the whole thing, nothing new to us. That's how the War Between the States was fought where I came from. There was no law on our farmlands but what strong men provided. Days were long and nights were short, and we made the best use of our time where any secessionists were concerned. The stories I was raised on I can't repeat, for obvious reasons. We managed our communities properly through that terrible conflict, but afterwards the Republicans got so used to running things that they took all the gravy and left little bits of slop for all the rest of us.

I became disgusted and moved the whole family to Florida in 1881, a land that was fresh and untamed and where prosperity was on the table for a newcomer to enjoy. I found my Bee Ridge place, and the neighbors, what few there were, welcomed me, the first doctor that some had ever seen.

By and large, our small community was hard-working and honest. I persuaded my brother-in-law to move in from Kansas. Not that it took much persuading. He was tired of Republican corruption, too, and in Manatee County a young man with legal inclinations could become a lawyer in no time. Before you knew it he wasn't just "Bart" but he was Justice of the Peace William Bartholomew.

One by one, I met the others in the Sarasota Vigilance Society, upright men determined to build something solid and new upon this vast rich tropical goldmine. Just as in Iowa, there are dirty elements here in Sarasota. They want a say in everything, mostly to the detriment of an honest man, and they tolerate the lowest forms of life who will support them. People do unspeakable things when they don't fear God or man and live so far from either one that they don't think anyone is watching. Well, we started to watch.

Before it was over, as I came to find out during the course of my apprehension of the criminals, this outlaw crusade against Abbe turned darker than any normal person could have anticipated.

Not all of the cases being tried at Pine Level were trivial. One of Postmaster Abbe's better customers, a country landowner named Tip Riley, was indicted on the serious charge of fornicating with a married woman. This was brought to the law's attention by the busybody with a gun, Dr. Leonard Andrews. The woman, Mary Surginer, denied the charge but was thoroughly shamed by such public exposure.

Ironically, Tip Riley's lawyer was Dr. Andrews' brother-in-law, William Bartholomew, the new lawyer and Justice of the Peace from Kansas. He succeeded in having the adultery charge dismissed, but soon the hapless woman died, possibly from humiliation and possibly from arsenic administered to induce an abortion. Tip Riley was then charged with her murder. His attorney, Bartholomew, switched sides and testified against him.

There always has been a shortage of honest lawyers hereabouts.

During a break in the murder trial, on a Monday morning, Riley took his customary ride to Sarasota to get his mail at the post office. Of several possible routes, he decided to follow the newly graded road from Bee Ridge to Postmaster Abbe's store. Halfway there, guns boomed and Tip Riley lay dead in the road, bushwhacked.

Two men did the deed; their plan was simple. They used a machete to hack out a place to squat, hiding in the saw palmettos, where they waited. When Tip Riley came along on his horse, they sprang and fired at him from ten feet away. That knocked him out of the saddle. Still alive, he got to his knees in the dirt. One of the killers rushed from hiding, pulled Riley's head back by his hair and used the machete to slit his throat, finishing the grisly job.

Hours passed before Riley's horse found its way home with pellets of shot in its head and .22 punctures throughout its body. The young Riley boy, who saw the wounded horse, ran to the neighbors yelling that someone had shot his daddy. The farmers were roused to locate the body, which they soon did, and then kept watch over it until the law could get there.

The law was not particularly swift. Riley's neighbors spent a long hot day and then a long night waiting for it. Riley got stiff, and the men built a fire to keep the flies off him. When the law finally arrived, it came in the person of William Bartholomew, the victim's one-time attorney, one-time accuser, and now acting in his capacity as Justice of the Peace. He showed up early in the morning, and found himself facing a group of hard-looking armed men, red-eyed from lack of sleep, guarding a corpse.

ISAAC REDD'S STORY

They invited my son Theodore to join the so-called Democratic club, which I came to learn was actually the Sarasota Vigilance Society. He asked me what I thought about it. I have fought in two wars, first against Billy Bowlegs in the Seminole War and second against the whole Yankee army in front of Richmond. I have been a warrior for Florida. Now I am a warrior for the Lord.

I told him "No!"

Theodore is young, 23-years old, and headstrong. He has an infant boy of his own to raise already. Born a bastard. I encouraged Theodore to formalize his union to Adelaide in our church, and he finally manned up and did it.

And by the Lord's grace he escaped the lure of the vigilantes.

I heard the shots fired that Monday morning from a mile away. Theodore heard them, too, as he was preparing to ride off to our cow pens. I told him to pay no attention, just go on about his business, and thankfully he listened to me. After others found the poor scoundrel Tip Riley's corpse, Theodore, being considered an honest young man, was called upon to help investigate the scene of the crime, a crime in which he was absolutely not involved.

As he told it to me, he saw the deceased laying just on the edge of the road, face to the ground. His left arm was doubled beneath him, and the other arm was clutching a handful of grass. He was dead, naturally. Theodore located the palmettos where the killers had laid about four feet apart, on the left side of the road, going towards the post office. Shot had blown holes in the palmettos. You see, Theodore's investigation was thorough. He found two shotgun shells, one fired and one cut in half, and some wads. One of the other men found a piece of paper out on the prairie 100 yards away with blood on it, as if it had been used to clean a knife.

Theodore asked me to send for our Justice of the Peace, Will Bartholomew, and I did, but Bartholomew took his own sweet time. My son spent all night with the body, swatting away the bugs. After Bartholomew finally got there, and got his inquest concluded, Theodore decided for some reason to ride to Sarasota and go into Bidwell's store. There he saw a No. 12 breech-loading shotgun lying across the counter. Bidwell said it was his and put it away. And that, dear friends, is everything my son knows.

The formal inquest was held at the scene of the crime. Riley's boy Marcus and his cousin stood quietly to one side under a tree. The dead man's widow was not in attendance. The day was a scorcher, and Justice of the Peace Bartholomew sweated heavily under his black coat. Clearing his throat, he rallied to call the inquest to order in his loud courtroom voice. Testimony was taken from those who had found the body. Or perhaps no one spoke and the formalities of the inquest were only in the recollections of those who later testified at trial, because eventually there was a trial. In any case, when the inquest was all done, Bartholomew studied the circle of implacable faces, nodded as if he had reached a profound conclusion and pronounced Riley dead, by persons unknown. He next announced his authority for the man to be buried and then got back onto his horse. That was the end of Tip Riley's story on this planet Earth.

But it did not take long for speculators to appear, pestering Tip Riley's grieving widow about selling her farm.

MARCUS RILEY'S STORY

    Daddy knew there were people after him. We kept a gun and a pistol loaded. One was by his bed and one was by mine. He nailed shutters over the windows in the back. He wanted them to have to come at him from the front. Where our house is, there's woods on three sides, but the front yard would give us a clear field of fire. That's why the murdering cowards had to bushwhack him on the road.

    The way daddy was left, dead in the dirt, his body was face downwards but he was up on his knees with his arms out like he was trying to crawl away. Most of his face was blowed off, his coat was almost cut to pieces, and his throat was cut from one end to the other.

    You might imagine how hard it was to get him straightened out enough to bury.

    One thing I'd like to know is, how did they know he'd be riding that way to town on that Monday morning? Who was watching him?

CHAPTER THREE
CHRISTMAS

It was Christmas Eve, still 1884, and Clarinda Barlow knew something was wrong as soon as Pa stumbled into the house.

"Been drinking," he said, and she could smell enough on him to know what that meant. He would crash around the cabin and finally fall down and go to sleep. This had gotten to be a regular occurrence. It had been almost a year since his wife had left.

But on this night, he got up close to her, and reached out an arm to touch her, but not quite. And said, "You're too pretty for this place. And way too smart."

"Shut up and get out of here, Pa," Clarinda ordered.

"I'm pleased you're as bright as you are," he said, and sat down hard. "Brains can take a woman a long ways," he added.

She went on about her business, cleaning up the small room. The only light came from a hanging lantern with its oil running low.

"This ain't been good for you." Pa gestured at their living quarters from his resting spot on the floor. "I know that. But you're the queen of this place now, and I'll fight for you, no matter what."

"Thank you, Pa. I know you will." She wondered how good he would really be if there were trouble. For example, there was that fool Charley Willard always sneaking around, afraid to show himself to Pa but only too ready to show himself to her. He was pure trash, as her mama would have said. He'd come riding around every month or so, usually cross-eyed with drink. Did the feller even work, she wondered? He'd tie his horse in the bushes and then try to sneak up on her just to scare her when she was walking by herself in the yard or tending to the cow.

"You married yet?" That was Willard's favorite line, and he'd say it with his high-pitched laugh, showing off a mouthful of pearly white teeth under his mustache. That was his only good feature in her opinion. Otherwise he was nothing but long nasty black hair, too many whiskers, lots of sweaty clothes and a bulge in his pants. Usually he'd smell like whiskey, too, and drinking was probably all that he did when he was having fun gallivanting around through the pines and the scrub jungle, twenty or thirty miles from where he was supposed to be.

She didn't like Willard one bit, but it was a diversion having someone come around and pay attention to her. Other than him, their grand society consisted of a cowboy now and again looking to cull a few head from the wild herds that still roamed free on the prairie, and, occasionally, some other family on the move, looking for a handout, people just as poor as the Barlow's. Nobody ever stayed.

"Just cause you ain't married doesn't mean you have to wait for it,"

Willard would croon in a sing-song voice. "You can still enjoy a man's company of an evening, darlin'."

He'd tell her what a big man he was back home in Sarasota, all lies, she thought. But she believed him when he told her how dangerous he could be, if and when he wanted to be. He had a mean look in his eye, and he carried a whip and a cheap shiny pistol.

But the final straw was that he had come close to seeing her naked. There was a spring, a sweet depression, in the woods near the Barlow home place where white-star-rushes, rain lilies and yellow pitcher plants grew. It was not so much larger than Clarinda was herself, but it was cool, and on occasion she had stripped off her worn farm duds and slid into the water. She never stayed long, since it was hard to suspend concerns about snakes and salamanders for more than a few minutes, but even the brief immersion was refreshing. One hot afternoon, it was Christmas Eve, just as she was unbuttoning her flannel shirt, she heard a twig snap and looked around to find that calloused Willard rube grinning at her from behind a tree. He took a step forward, and she shrieked. But that's not what stopped him. He suddenly yelped and toppled over backwards. As she ran away she saw what had scared him: a black snake coiled by his feet.

"It just surprised me a little," Willard called after her as he was getting up and dusting off his pants. "And how'd you like some wiggly ol' snake up your drawers?"

She rushed into the house to get her scattergun, planning to run Willard off in a hurry, but by the time she hurried back outside he was already riding away. He reined up at the edge of the woods to wave his hat at her and holler something she couldn't understand. But she heard him laughing his high funny laugh as he spurred off down the trail. She was overcome by a wave of revulsion and shame. How could she ever feel clean again?

"Oh, Lord," she prayed. "Please don't let Charley Willard be the best that I can do!"

Later that night, that very same Christmas Eve, young Charley Willard camped out in the woods, his boots pointed to the fire. He was feeling sorry for himself and his sorry life. He had always been treated unfairly, by school teachers who resented his smart tongue, despite his good looks; by his mother who had run off and deserted him; by his father who lost a foot in the War and got sent to prison over a gambling dispute; by every straw boss who had ever fired him; and now by this girl, Clarinda, who thought she was too good for him. To make matters worse, he was out of booze.

It was some solace to him that he was well-regarded by certain very important people. He had friends in Sarasota who had grand ideas, rock-solid plans, who would shake this whole stinking place up, and they wanted him to be right by their side. Trusted him, in fact, to take care of this mighty important business in the very near future. "And the first shall be last," he said to himself. "And the other way around," he mumbled, then snored.

Christmas Day was celebrated by the Abbe family in Sarasota with a beef roast and a Bible reading. They had dinner with the Whitakers who lived on the bayou named for their family. The eldest Abbe daughter, Nellie, had married Furman Whitaker. The Whitakers were the original settlers of the area, arriving before the War Between the States. It was said that the fugitive, Judah P. Benjamin, deposed Secretary of State and War for the Lost Cause, had hidden with the Whitakers on his hazardous and successful escape from the Yankee horse soldiers, a trip that would eventually take him all the way to Cuba, then on to England and a new career.

The Whitakers had acquired a lot of acreage. They also had a good business shipping mullet roe to Cuba. (Mullet by the millions swam in our bays and their tidal tributaries, leaping about in such great number that steering a sailboat through dense schools of them could be quite dangerous. They could alter a vessel's course or, so it was said, even swamp a boat by jumping aboard.)

Compared to the Whitakers, Postmaster Abbe's family was almost poor folks, and they were Republicans, which was an anathema to some of the "pioneer" families who had endured the privations of the war. But Manatee County, stretching a hundred miles south from the broad river for which it was named, was so sparsely populated that politics were driven by intense community issues rather than by national party banners.

When the Abbes got to Florida much of the land south of the Manatee and Braden Rivers was nearly free for the taking. It could be acquired for homesteading for a dollar and twenty-five cents an acre or bought by quitclaim for less than that. Charles Abbe and his wife Charlotte were well situated to take advantage of that since he had been successful in business. As a self-educated horticulturalist, he preached the principles of progressive agriculture. He also believed that the future of South Florida was in real estate, especially in fertile property that could be developed into citrus farms. He was not alone – there was a lot of that sentiment in the air. Before long, in addition to buying Florida land, Abbe was traveling around the Midwest extolling the benefits of Florida produce at agricultural fairs held in places like Anderson, Indiana, where there were prospective buyers for his fruit and also prospective settlers for this unfolding promised land in the last American frontier (promising now that the Indians had been subdued).

Mr. Abbe's store opened on what would come to be the main street of town, and he won the rights to be its first postmaster. Since the government favored post offices with only a single name, it was Abbe who turned Sara Sota into Sarasota, and nobody seemed to mind. The inhabitants were pleased with a regular delivery of mail by the schooners and steamers that ran down from Tampa and Cedar Key once a week in good weather.

Two days after their Christmas meal at the Whitakers, on a December morning so brisk and clear that just breathing the air invigorated the body, Postmaster Abbe got up and skipped breakfast to go down to the beach. His day's task was to pull his small sailboat out of the water to give the hull a scraping and a fresh coat of paint. He now owned about three hundred acres of prime bayfront north and south of Hudson Bayou. To his eyes – and to those of everyone who came and saw it – this was just about the prettiest place in the whole world, with sapphire blue water, glistening white sand, and a vast sunny sky covered with flocks of sea birds – thousands of them. Especially in winter the birds came through, waves of white egrets and ibis, roseate spoonbills, herons of all sorts, pelicans, eagles and migratory ducks and songbirds. There were osprey plucking fish from the bay and so many kinds of wading birds pecking for food along the beach that they were really underfoot. Around the Abbe home you almost had to duck for the hummingbirds, bright red cardinals, and the many-hued buntings and jays. The sky was ruled by bald eagles, and the mangrove islands were crowded roosts for fat brown and white pelicans. Woodpeckers whacked away at the trees in the backyard and frightening great horned owls hooted all night. In Abbe's mind it was as close to heaven as he was going to get.

Abbe was carefully sliding his brush along the wooden bow of his fishing craft when a man approached. It was Charley Willard, the very same Charley Willard who was troubling young Clarinda back in the bush. Charley was a neighbor of Abbe's and usually stayed with some woman about a mile to the south. It was clear he'd already been drinking – probably sugarcane moonshine called *aguardente*.

Willard and Abbe didn't get along, or not get along. Running a store, especially one with a post office, Abbe got to know a lot about people. Customers, of necessity, revealed their finances and their business connections, and a storekeeper had the chance to talk with them about all manner of things – to gossip really. Willard, however, generally traded at Alfred Bidwell's store, not at Abbe's, so the two were not that well connected. But, like they say, everybody in a small town knows everybody else's business.

Willard greeted Abbe cordially enough, "Looks like you're working hard." He was swaying slightly, doubtless an effect of the liquor.

"There's always lots to do. What brings you over here, Charley?"

Down the wide path to the beach, coming through the cabbage palms, another man appeared, Charles Morehouse, who had just arrived from Illinois on Christmas Eve. It had taken him a several days' journey by train and schooner to vacation with the Abbes. Now he observed Abbe and Willard in conversation and started to walk into the sun to join them. The strange cries and singing of the wild birds made it impossible to hear what was being said by the pair beside the boat, but Morehouse did see their conversation suddenly become quite animated.

Willard actually poked Abbe in the chest. The Christmas visitor paused, not wanting to intrude in a private matter. He saw Abbe stand up, paint brush in hand, and yell something in the other's face.

Willard broke it off and strode across the beach back in the direction he had come, toward Alfred Bidwell's store with its dock protruding to the water. Charles Morehouse decided it was time to make himself known and crossed the sand.

"What was that about?" he asked Abbe.

"That ornery dumb ass wanted to talk about the election. He's so proud that Cleveland won. Though I doubt he's even qualified to vote. I tried to be nice and told him I thought Cleveland would be all right. Nothing Earth-shaking about it. Everybody deserves a turn, but Willard didn't like that answer."

"What did he want you to say?"

"No telling. He just wanted a fight. The man's drunk and it's not even noon." Abbe wrapped his brush in a rag.

"Still on a Christmas Day high?" Morehouse suggested.

"Could be. There was a big party over at Bidwell's store, or behind it at Dr. Hunter's. You could hear it from here. They all got liquored up from that still they think is hid in the palmettos. Anyway, I'm hungry now and this paint needs to dry. Let's walk back to the house."

Abbe stowed the tools in a wheelbarrow and pushed it up the beach, leaving a long straight line crossing the sand and a carpet of seashells. Moorhouse took a moment to inspect a sand dollar, a novelty to him, then hurried to catch up.

A road, that Abbe had himself laid out, began at a row of palm trees all of which bent inland, turned from the sea by years of prevailing westerly winds.

Morehouse stopped abruptly and pointed at some figures who seemed to be crouched near their path in a stand of saw palmettos and rosemary bushes. "What are they up to over there?" he asked. "Is that two, maybe three, men?"

Abbe gave it a quick glance and said, "No business of mine." There were always things going on in this tropical outpost that were best to ignore.

Yet one of the men suddenly rose up and pointed a gun. "Abbe!" he yelled and immediately let loose with both of the gun's double barrels.

Kablam! Kablam! It deafened Morehouse and sent screeching birds flapping away like the storm of shot had hit them.

Most of Abbe's head blew off, and his hat sailed the other way.

Morehouse crouched on the path in shock, with no way to run. He saw Charley Willard emerge from the bushes and approach, holding his shotgun level with Morehouse's face. Was the gun still loaded? That question raced through his mind.

"Are you killing me?" Morehouse asked desperately.

"Are you one of them?" Willard demanded.

Morehouse cried, "No! I'm a visitor here!"

"Then I ain't killing you," Willard said, blessing him with life. "You just git!"

Morehouse made for the wheelbarrow handles, thinking vaguely of taking the tools back to the house where they belonged. His friend's blood was pouring onto the sand. Most of his face was gone.

"Run while you can," Willard warned. The boy's face was flushed – at twenty-three, Willard was just an overgrown, red-faced boy - but Morehouse complied. He backed up the path, facing Willard, expecting to be shot. Then he turned and ran.

"I ain't got no more shells anyhow," Willard said, looking down at Abbe's body, chest down with the blood draining away. He spat, waiting for the approval of his friends.

Another neighbor, clipping suckers off the tomato vines by his house, heard the blasts.

"That was Joe Anderson's gun," he said to his wife. "What do you suppose he's shooting at?"

His wife, bent over on the other side of the row, said, "The way that second barrel goes off whenever he pulls the first trigger, whatever he was aiming at won't be moving anytime soon. Unless he was too drunk to hit anything. They've been partying for two days."

"Now, darlin'," her husband admonished her.

Down the road, Abbe's wife, Charlotte, had heard the shots, too, and rushed out to the front porch to investigate. Morehouse came running on the trail. He bounded up the steps. A cold sweat broke over her body and her knees buckled. She knew. Somehow she just knew.

"They shot Mister Abbe!" she screamed before he could speak.

Morehouse nodded, gasping for breath. The frantic widow rushed past him down the road to her husband's body. Inexplicably, it was gone, nowhere to be found, not then, not ever.

In the distance, at water's edge, three men pushed a little skiff off the beach; one jumped aboard, and the skiff sailed off, disappearing across the calm waters of Sarasota Bay.

CHAPTER FOUR

THE LONG RIDE

Now we get to the story I want to tell, the part when I became involved in these unfortunate affairs. It was my first experience as a lawman, and it came that very same fateful day, two days after Christmas, 1884. I happened to be calling on Captain Duff, in answer to his summons to join his family for a big hog roast. It was my birthday. I had turned eighteen years old, and I judged myself to be a grown man. I sure could eat like one, and I was out to prove it. Just watching smoke rise out of that pit, smelling the pig fat dripping into the coals, I was right where I wanted to be for the rest of my life.

Lemuel Duff was his true name, but nobody ever called him anything but "Captain" in tribute to his wartime service with John Tyler Morgan's Alabama Cavalry, about which I had heard many tales that also featured my late father, Wallace MacFarlane. He was one of that company – and a major at that – along with Duff and the third hero of those stories, the man who raised me, our Manatee County Sheriff,

A.J. "Sandy" Watson. I lived on the Watson farm growing up, while the sheriff made his home "in town," which to us meant Manatee City, also called Braidentown, then Bradentown, then Bradenton. It's all the same place. I'll just call it by its old name, Manatee City.

The pig was getting nearly done, and we were all squatting around the fire waiting to have a little test bite, when up gallops Sheriff Watson with the news that the postmaster down in Sarasota had been shot dead right by his house. "We need to ride down there right now, men!" he ordered.

Captain Duff was also a deputy sheriff and needed to go. But when I heard "men," I realized I was being invited along. And was I game!

"Grab a chunk of that pork," Duff instructed me, and the sheriff, "and we'll ride." We made quick work of half the pig, lifting off the tin, lifting it out of the coals, and lopping off some choice pieces. Mrs. Duff hurried out of the house to provide us with brown paper bags to stuff the meat in. She said she and her girls would tend to the rest of the pig, and she'd expect her husband back by morning. She also fixed me a little pack with a blanket in it, and a knife and fork. As I remember it, she also put in some fried flour biscuits and a box of salt.

This was high times - off on a posse! I had my sorrel horse Whistler and a big pistol strapped to the saddle, and I was riding hard with the strong men of our community representing the law, for fifteen miles on a well-worn road. The sheriff wore a black, flat-brimmed preacher's hat. I had one like it, only mine was tan.

I don't think I had ever been to Sarasota before, but Sheriff Watson knew the way to Abbe's post office and store. About six hours had passed since the poor man was shot, and it was beginning to get dark.

We dismounted at the murder scene. There were a lot of excited people standing on the path to show us the way to where the killing had been done. A group of men and boys were there, waiting for the law to arrive. In the midst of them was the spot where Abbe had fallen. The sand was stained with his blood. Someone picked up Abbe's hat where it had been blown from his head and handed it to the sheriff. The body was gone, but we were shown a trail of blood leading toward the beach.

The sheriff and Captain Duff followed the path, and I stayed as close to them as I could. A number of the townsfolk joined in behind, whispering among themselves. It was near sunset.

A man who identified himself as Charles Morehouse, a Christmas visitor, was waiting for us at the beach. He was pacing at the edge of the rippling waves and watching the early moon rise. He confirmed that the murderer was Charley Willard, which was the name we had been hearing.

"It happened right in front of me," Morehouse reported. "He killed Mr. Abbe in cold blood, for no reason, with no remorse. Astonishing!" Morehouse still had the shakes. "Willard stood right in front of me," he repeated, pointing his finger at the sheriff, "close as we are right now. He could have shot me but he didn't. He asked me if I was one of them, and I said no. I have no idea who 'them' is. Then he let me go. I saw others in the bushes," Morehouse gestured at the greenery on the dunes, "but I can't say who they were."

"Where's this Willard live?" the sheriff asked the expanding assembly around us.

"With Chandler Yonge," someone piped up. "The boy's also got a fiancé about a mile from here, past Bidwell's store. That's where he mostly stays. But it won't do any good to go there. He lit out on his horse a couple hours ago."

"Going where?" the sheriff asked. The man shrugged.

"It was Joe Anderson's gun I heard," another neighbor volunteered. "There ain't another one that fires twice every time you pull off a shot."

I walked along the beach while they talked and found a shallow trench that could have been made by a boat hull. I waved at the sheriff. He came over to look and spotted something I hadn't seen, footprints, some made by a person without any shoes.

"Get back!" he ordered the onlookers. "We got footprints here to inspect."

Captain Duff bent down to read what he could in the sand. Having done so, he conjectured that more than one man had dragged the body to the water, and that more than one man, or woman, had launched a boat from the beach.

"There's something odd about these bare feet," he declared. Sheriff Watson and I looked closely to try to see what that was, and the sheriff got it first. "That man's left foot is skinnier than his right," he said. And as he delivered that conclusion, a wave came over and erased everything we were looking at.

"If we catch anybody I guess we can make them take off their shoes and see," the sheriff said pensively. "But I'm very sorry we can't give the widow the peace of mind of finding her husband's body." It was dark by then, too late for searching.

"We'll start again in the morning and form up a better posse," Sheriff Watson said, "and we'll make camp over there," he pointed to Bidwell's dock. "But keep an eye out for that boat. It might come back."

He asked for volunteers among the men had been guarding the scene and appointed a number of deputies. Some of them decided to camp out with us, and a cluster of small campfires arose where the palm trees met the beach. The neighbors helped us with water and feed for our horses and offered us food. We gratefully accepted some oranges and cans of beans, but we had our main course wrapped in the paper bags straight from the pig roast.

The three of us, me, the Captain and the sheriff, built our fire on the beach and enjoyed our feast. The dock from Bidwell's store loomed over us, highlighted by the moon. After he ate his fill, Captain Duff decided to climb up on the dock for a little breeze. He sat there quietly smoking, looking across the water at the long black streaks of clouds drifting toward the north. No boats appeared on the dark water, and the Captain finally climbed down to sack out on a blanket he spread over the sand. "See you about daybreak," he grunted, adding hopefully, "Body might wash up with the tide."

I sat with the sheriff at fireside sipping hot coffee, just like a man. And like men we talked about fishing.

"Plenty of snook out there," I'd say.

"And mackerel, pompano, redfish," he'd say. "All we need is a hook and a net."

When that conversation ran down, Sheriff Watson stared up at the stars. In time he cleared his throat and began a little speech he must have been preparing in his mind. "Gawain," he started, "being that today is your eighteenth birthday I think I ought to say a few things despite the bad events that have brought us here tonight. You know your pap and I grew up together up in Alabama. We was tight, like that!" The sheriff held up his fist. The flickering fire gave him an angry look.

That much I knew.

"Wallace and I even loved the same girl. Your ma. And your dad got her." This was news to me. The sheriff was silent for a moment. "How about some more coffee?"

He meant for himself. I had to push the pot around where he could more easily reach the handle.

"Wallace and me joined up together with John Tyler Morgan's Cavalry, like a lot of the other men we'd grown up with. If you had a horse they were happy to enlist you. Both me and your dad had fine mounts we were quite proud of. I was planning on stealing a pistol from my father, but the cavalry issued me one just as good or better. Lord, Gawain, me and your dad fought together all over Mississippi and Tennessee." He paused to reflect for a moment before resuming. "There was nothin' but battles, son, from beginning to end. We were in a fight every couple of days it seemed like. It's surprising anybody survived what we went through. Wallace, he could sure shoot."

"I can shoot, too," I reminded him. I often felt that my talents went unnoticed, and, truly, I even surprised myself at how good my marksmanship was.

"Yes, you can shoot," he conceded. "You're pretty much dead-on with that ol' 'Peacemaker' you carry." He was referring to a well-used Army pistol, a Colt .45 six-shooter, that I had inherited from my father and treasured.

"I could do a lot with that with that .30-30 Winchester repeater you carry," I told him.

"That, too," the sheriff laughed. "But you'll have to earn a rifle like mine."

"I'll do it," I boasted, and was ready to say more about myself but I teared up when a breeze caused the smoke to drift right into my eyes.

"I'm sure you will," he agreed. "Anyway, what I wanted to say was how much I miss your ma and your pa both."

"She died when I was born."

"That's right, son. Nothing you can do about it."

"And my pa drank himself to death or killed hisself. So I've been told."

The dark night hid the sheriff's reaction to those words, but he said, "I'd like to know who told you that, Gawain. Your dad was just about the bravest man I ever saw. He charged straight into a Yankee breastworks at Chickamauga. He got shot off his horse, and the horse died, but the men rallied behind your dad and put those Yankees on a run. Wallace never did get over the wounds which took out most of his insides. He was in terrible, terrible pain all the time after that, so I'd say the War killed him. I don't know how he lasted as many years after the surrender as he did."

"I was four when he died."

"That's right. Born two days after Christmas in 1866. Your dad did what he could to raise you, and…"

"It was you and Miz' Watson who raised me," I insisted, though in actuality they had put me out on their farm to be raised by the Ephrams.

"That's true, too. May the Lord rest my wife's soul. And I'd say you've turned out well, Gawain. Your dad was made out of rawhide and you're about half rawhide yourself. Now I know we didn't have much of a Christmas celebration this week. I guess that'll just have to wait. But I do have something for you. Something that your father left in my safekeeping." He dug into his jacket. "There's this…"

He handed me a shiny gold coin. "That's an 1870 Liberty Head twenty-dollar gold piece. You keep that in your pocket until you need something important. And there's this book, too." He passed a small volume across the fire.

I studied the coin and how it glowed in the firelight, and I slid it into my pants. On the cover of the book there was a picture of a man, and the title was "The Songs from Robert Burns."

"Poems," I said doubtfully.

"Yessir, that's what it is," the sheriff acknowledged. "I figured out that much myself. Now I don't get too much out of poetry, but your pa would pull that book out and read from it when we was camping on the ground on that long campaign through Tennessee, and it was very restful, very beautiful to listen to."

"Then I guess I'm supposed to read it." I wasn't exactly delighted with the prospect.

"I think so, and maybe it'll give you some comfort like it did to us. Anyway, that's what he wanted me to give you. I held 'em in safe keeping." The sheriff's speech was done.

"I don't think I'll read it now though," I said. I had read a book about King Arthur and his Round Table, but never a book of poems, or songs.

"No, it's too late to read. Let's catch some 'shut eye.' Tomorrow we're going to catch some men."

"On whatever terms they choose to be caught," the sheriff added, and he laid back to look at the stars.

That night I dreamt about John Tyler Morgan's Cavalry, slashing and dashing through Tennessee on their gallant and bloody missions into history. And in my dreams they always won.

Before daybreak we made our coffee and had a breakfast of last night's pig leftovers. As soon as there was light to see, we made a more thorough search of the beach but failed to find anything of interest. The sheriff requisitioned all of the skiffs and rowboats we could see and had them out searching Sarasota Bay for Mr. Abbe's body and even out to the keys as far as Long Boat. While that was going on, we rode out to call upon one Joe Anderson, who had been identified as the owner of the murder weapon – a double-barreled shotgun that fired both barrels when you pulled either trigger.

We found him at his log cabin on the road north to Osprey. He had evidently been expecting a formal visit because, despite the early hour, he came to the door fully dressed and freshly shaved. About the shooting, he professed to know nothing.

"Zero!" he said, shaking his head.

When asked to produce his shotgun he looked sad, "I don't have it. Charley Willard borrowed it. Didn't say what for. He ain't brought it back yet."

"We've got a witness who says there were other men who took part in the ambush," the sheriff explained. "Two or three were seen lurking in the bushes. Was one of them you?" He raised his voice. "I've heard the name Ed Bacon from some of your neighbors. Was he one, too?"

Anderson denied it all, almost crying. "I'd like to know what neighbor of mine said what," he whined.

"I'm taking you with us," the sheriff informed him. "Have you got a horse?"

Anderson did, and he was made to ride with we lawmen another mile to Willard's girlfriend's cottage on the same road.

A thin pale woman who looked like a school teacher came to the door, and the first thing she said was, "He's not here." I imagine she had heard what her fiancé had done and was more terrified of him than of us.

The sheriff dismounted. "How'd you know we were looking for Mr. Willard?" he asked.

"Well, aren't you? You're a lawman and there's no other reason you'd come around here. Is Charley dead?"

"Not that I know of ma'am, but you're right. It's him we want. Where is he?"

"I don't know," she said, jaw clenched so firmly her words could be barely heard. "He doesn't live here, sir. We're engaged but not married. I haven't seen him since noon yesterday when he took his horse and rode off." She straightened her skirt with tiny hands and started to close the door.

"Rode off to where?" the sheriff asked, persisting.

"Wherever he took a notion to." She sounded exasperated. "He doesn't tell me those things. Or much else," she added.

"Mind if we look around inside?" Captain Duff asked.

"I certainly do mind. You can't come snooping around a woman's home without some papers."

"I don't agree with you there," the sheriff told her. "But to ease your sensibilities we'll just send in the boy, only to make sure your man, I mean fiancé, hasn't sneaked back in."

I jumped off Whistler and brushed by the woman, just like I was a full-fledged deputy. She didn't put up a fight. Inside were three rooms, and a quick look in each, and under the bed, told me no one was hiding. The place was tidy. There was a photograph of a good-looking man on the dresser. I would remember that face.

I told the sheriff it was clear, and he hoisted himself back into the saddle. "You let us know if he comes back, ma'am. You know we want him for murdering Postmaster Abbe. He can turn himself in and things might go better for him."

She didn't say a word, just stared at us.

Riding away I told the sheriff, "There was one strange thing in that house. A chair with a broken leg was leaned up against their table, like maybe there had been a fight. Also, there was a pile of ladies' clothes and a suitcase on the bed. Do you think she plans to join Willard?"

"If that's her intention she'll be disappointed," the sheriff said, "because we're going to catch up with him before very long. But I doubt that's her plan." He slowed his horse to address the prisoner Anderson, who was riding glumly behind him, followed by Captain Duff who had a rifle resting across his knees. "Don't Willard have people out by the Myakka River?" he asked.

"He's got a brother somewheres," Anderson responded reluctantly.

"Yeah. I believe I have an idea where he lives," the sheriff said. "I expect that's the first place Willard would run to."

We rode back to Sarasota where the sheriff wanted to deliver his condolences to Mrs. Abbe. Her house was one of the best in town. It even had an upstairs, with a dozen big windows and white painted siding. It was set back in a grove of moss-covered live oak trees.

The sheriff walked up on the wide porch while I, with Captain Duff, guarded Joe Anderson out by the road. But at the door, Mr. Morehouse, the unfortunate murder witness, told the sheriff that Mrs. Abbe was resting in bed and not receiving guests.

"Please tell her I came by to express my sorrow at her loss," I heard Sheriff Watson say.

The sheriff came back, and he addressed the posse. He had decided that in the morning he would escort Anderson up to the jail in Manatee City, being that the jail at the new courthouse in Pine Level was too far away and might not have a guard in attendance. "But we'll have it ready for Willard when we catch him," he shouted. "And they'll want to clear off the brush around their hanging tree." There was such a tree, but it had never been used for a legal execution – only lynchings. I suppose the sheriff made mention of it only for Joe Anderson's benefit.

He put Captain Duff in charge of our volunteers and said they were to set off as a posse after Charley Willard. He handed the Captain a pocketful of badges and started to give directions to Willard's brother's house, but one of the men in the posse said he knew the way.

Then, to my surprise, Sheriff Watson looked at me and said, "Gawain, what do you want to do?"

Well, hell! I told him I'd ride with Captain Duff and the posse.

"Good enough," he said. He instructed Captain Duff to pick up what supplies he thought we needed at Abbe's store, "and tell whoever's there to send me a bill. Get enough for a couple of days. You'll ride out at first light and catch that scoundrel as quickly as possible. And take Gawain along. He might make himself useful and will certainly benefit from the experience."

CHARLEY WILLARD'S STORY

How could I be as bad as they say? Didn't I tell old Bidwell and Alford to leave Tip Riley alone? There was no way to take that old man out safely. His cabin was way back in the woods with a clear range of fire to the front. He had dogs that would warn him of anybody sneaking up behind his house, and probably had hogs and bear traps out there and everything else. There was probably alligators and snakes, too. And Riley's boy knows how to shoot. I've seen him do it.

Dr. Andrews said he wanted to give Riley a good thrashing, and I said no, not me. If we beat him up he'll come here and cut my gizzard right in my own bed.

So then what happens? The word comes down – from where I don't know – they said it was from the "leadership" - that Tip wouldn't be beaten but must be killed instead. And I was supposed to go and wait for him at the horse ford we call Brown's Crossing at such and such a time on such and such a morning. Jason Alford and that Adam Hunter were to go over to Phillippi Creek in case Riley went that way, and Ed Bacon and Lewis Cato were to go over to the Bee Ridge Road and wait. Whichever way Riley went, we'd have it covered. And what for? To kill one useless son of a bitch? Who never made any problem with me?

Abbe? Now that's another thing. There's good people in my family. We own property on Little Sarasota Bay and down in Horse and Chaise. But there sure ain't any money to be made in Sarasota, and who's to blame for that? Postmaster Abbe! He had more than his share of the land, and all the land. Way too much! And he always looked down on me.

Hard to believe that I damn near blowed old Abbe's head clear off his neck! I sure as hell did! I guess I got 'er done! I sure enough guess I got 'er done!

But to be honest about it, I didn't hate the man. I still don't. Fact is, I don't even recall killing him, but I don't want that spread around. I was drunk on my ass. Go git him! Bidwell or someone said. You're a god damned officer in the "society." Do your job or take your punishment! You took the oath, Charley! I remember that much. And off went Abbe's head!

Well, nothing I can do about that now, is there? The deed is done. The cards is played. Keep on breathin' air, that's the name of the game, my dad said, and that's my ambition.

CHAPTER FIVE

CAPTAIN DUFF

Lemuel Duff, the Captain, wasn't a full-time deputy sheriff. He ran a lumberyard in Bradentown, selling mostly pine boards and timbers fresh from his own sawmill. He air-dried them so they were slow to warp and would hold a coat of paint. The lumber market was good and had nowhere to go but up, so he said. The big mills were stripping out acres and acres of native virgin pine trees, but there were countless miles of forest yet to log. People were coming, so he said, and they all needed houses.

I knew that the Captain was very happy to be called into service by the sheriff. Whenever hard-riding was necessary and a shootout might be possible, his response was always the same. He would load up his guns, put on the old slouch hat he had worn during the War, put his foreman and daughters in charge of the yard, and kiss his wife goodbye. (Sheriff Sandy Watson kidded Duff for being on his third wife. It wasn't really funny. The first had divorced him when he came back from the War crazy as a rooster, she said, which meant he wanted to lay everything in sight. His second wife didn't count because she got a drinking habit, mostly from Captain Duff, and fell off a boat and drowned in the Chattahoochee River. That was back in Alabama.) It made the Captain feel young, just to see his horse quiver when he slapped the saddlebags on and fit his "campaign boots" into the stirrups.

After the drowning Duff had moved south to Florida, lured there by his friend Sandy Watson, of course, who had also moved down from Alabama first to try his hand at farming. Watson had boasted about the boom times coming to the Florida frontier, and Duff needed some of that. This is how the Captain explained it to me.

When he got to Manatee County he still had a little savings that he'd managed not to drink up, and he went to work building houses. That got him into the lumber business. He got sober, mostly.

Things worked out well for Captain, and also for Sandy Watson who decided when he was about forty to ride his wartime record, his military bearing, and his silver hair into the sheriff's office. By that time, he had five kids of his own and me out on the farm, and a good wife. Sadly she died from malaria not too long after he got elected.

Captain Duff had lucked out on his third marriage, and the wife he found in Florida was the keeper. She seemed to like him fine. Ellen was her name, and she gave him two daughters. He was a lot tamer than he had been as a young man, but still nothing could please his disposition more than to buckle up his six-shooter and ride. It was my good fortune that Captain Duff also liked me.

CHAPTER SIX

REMEMBERING HOW I WAS RAISED

When I grew up, Sheriff Watson lived in town with his wife and multiple children but, like I said before, I was sent to live in the country. This was because I was an orphan and not one of the Watsons' own. My quarters consisted of a back stall in a barn. The Ephram family, Watson employees, did the hard work of clearing land, but were also helped out by Mister Sandy, as they called him, who was no shirker himself when it came to grubbing out palmettos and planting fruit trees. They had the only real house on the place, other than my barn - or warehouse we called it. I took my meals with the Ephrams and they saw to my needs, but a lot of the time I grew up by myself with the forest and the scrub prairie as my teachers. My evenings were spent watching the sunsets hidden behind soft green pine trees, and my sleep came with the love cries of frogs and distant panthers.

I got along fine with the Ephram kids, and with the Watson children for that matter, but the only true friend I had was Reuben, three years my senior. Reuben had been abandoned as a baby, so the story went, and been taken in by Mister and Missus Ephram. I asked Reuben how he got his name, and he didn't know. But the Ephrams are Biblical people, and the senior Mr. Ephram explained that according to his Bible, Reuben was cursed for sleeping with his father's mistress. So make of that what you will. Nevertheless, the Ephrams gave him their last name so that the boy would have a place in the world, though Ephram was locally considered to be a colored name. Reuben had the complexion of a Cuban, though in my opinion, he was as white as me.

We were both allowed to go together to the white school, on the rare occasions when we were made to go. Questions about Reuben's race and parentage, however, always made him easy pickings for the bigger boys, and luckily he grew up fast on his feet and quick with his fists. I'd have to admit that he was bigger, faster and stronger than me, but we shared a similar taste for adventure.

The rules at the Ephram home were loose. Once dinner was over and the chores done, Reuben was permitted to do as he pleased. I also ate with the family but slept a short hike away in the warehouse. I was the farm's night watchman so to speak. In reality, we were free to roam half the night, trapping for coons and rabbits and annoying the sleeping neighbors. I always did love roving about the country and learning its ways. Snakes, maybe because they were outcasts like me, became my favorite creatures, and I built up a sizable collection.

Mr. Ephram had a brother who lived in a shack down the road, and he had a young girlfriend who lived close by. Notwithstanding that she was supposed to be engaged to another man, these two sweethearts slipped out every chance they got. Reuben tracked them one evening to what he called their "love nest" in the lemon groves, where the air was always sweet and a breeze might keep the mosquitoes at bay. He ran back to the barn all excited to tell me that he'd seen "everything she had."

A week later here he came again, while I was reading my "Knights of the Round Table" book by candlelight, and said to forget the book and "come see the show." So we went crawling through the moist grass, and concealed ourselves behind a prickly lemon tree to observe the two lovers rolling about on a blanket. Brief glimpses of the girl's naked behind and ample breasts, illuminated by the moon, were my introduction to human sexual practices, though I was well acquainted with the behavior of farm animals.

"Ain't that something?" Reuben rejoiced when we got far enough away not to be heard.

I had to admit it was worth seeing.

CHAPTER SEVEN
THE POSSE

Our posse was now six men, counting me and Captain Duff. The other four were a horticulturalist named Piney Reasoner, who was building a pioneering citrus nursery; Mike, the blacksmith, who also created garden art out of plow parts; Furman Whitaker, son of the pioneer family and the husband of the Abbes' daughter Nellie; and Overton, a land surveyor. Basically, they had all been allies of the late Mr. Abbe and viewed themselves as the progressive and forward-looking element of the area.

It took more than three hours for us to ride through the dry pine forests and grass-covered scrub land to Willard's brother's house. We got lost a couple of times because our directions weren't so good after all. It was quite warm that afternoon despite the fact that it was the middle of winter.

We came across a few travelers, none of whom said they had heard about the Abbe murder, and one sweating farmer who was clearing a plot of land near the road with a young helper. They were using machetes and a mattock to grub out and uproot saw palmettos. The farmer heard us coming, straightened his sunburned shoulders, and walked up to meet us. He motioned for the boy to remain in the field. After making our introductions – his name was Cooper - he said he knew who Charley Willard was but declared he hadn't seen him recently. But he might have heard a rider pass through late the previous night.

"You mean he killed the postmaster?" The farmer seemed surprised. "Well, that's not the first senseless killing around here and it won't be the last. They ambushed Tip Riley last summer not five miles from here, and nobody ever did a thing about that."

"Who ambushed who?" Duff asked from the saddle.

"Tip Riley. Just some farmer. Can't say who did it. To hear some folks tell it he got caught out in the bushes with a woman not his wife, playing the game only two can play, if you get my meaning." The man winked and sniggered. "And they got found out. You hear lots of stories. Him and the postmaster was friends, or so I've been told by some people. Can't remember who exactly."

As they rode away Duff grumbled, "Strange how nobody ever can recall the actual name of who said what, when there's probably not more than fifty people living anywhere this side of the Myakka River."

It was approaching nightfall when we got near to what we believed to be Willard's brother's homestead. We tethered our tired horses out in the woods so we could sneak up on the house. We crawled through the bushes to surround the simple log cabin. Duff's plan was for us to hide until true dark and see who came in or out. Charley Willard might be inside.

It was uncomfortable laying there in the rough and swatting at bugs, but that's what we did. Finally, a lantern was lit inside. Other than that, and some farm animals stirring in a rude barn, nothing and nobody showed themselves inside, outside or around side.

"Don't they even use the outhouse?" the blacksmith, lying near me, complained.

Eventually the house went completely dark, which seemed to set off a racket of frogs and cicadas throughout the woods. I watched a family of raccoons sneak across the yard. The mama, big as a bear cub, was in front, followed by four kits. Finally, close to midnight, we'd all had enough of this, and Captain Duff gave us the signal to move in. We emerged from hiding with guns cocked.

Duff hit the front door and kicked it in. "We're the law!" he shouted.

A man bolted up in a bed. He had a gun on the blanket by his side, but he left it untouched. Also in bed with him was a child, who screamed. I struck a match to light a candle and gave a friendly wave to the kid, a girl, who retreated behind her pillow.

"You're Frank Willard, ain't ya?" Duff demanded.

"That's me." The man swung his legs onto the floor and retrieved his britches. "Don't guess I'm going to give you any fight since there's five or ten of you," he griped. "I ain't that stupid."

"That's good to know," Duff said. He ordered his deputies to go outside and search the grounds. I stayed in the house. Pistol in hand, I watched while Frank Willard buttoned his suspenders and straightened up and gathered a seat at his table. Captain Duff pulled up a chair across from him.

The girl turned out not to be so little when she got up and ran behind a curtain. I started to follow her, but Duff nodded it was okay, let her be.

Looking around the cabin, it was clear this particular Willard brother didn't own very much. A couple of tin plates and a wash bucket, one bed, a table and two chairs, summed up the entire inventory of his furnishings. The house had a dirt floor and palm fronds for a roof. These people down here are poor as pigs, was the thought that came to my mind.

"I'm Captain Duff," the conversation began. "We're after your brother Charley. He's killed a man in Sarasota."

"Is that right?" asked Willard's brother. He spread his hands, incredulous at this news. "Charley was here yesterday morning, but he didn't say anything about killing anybody."

"You don't seem much surprised by the possibility."

"Well, around here killin' ain't that uncommon," the man said. "Got a smoke?"

Duff shook his head. "What exactly did your brother say?"

"He wanted food and ammunition for his gun."

"A double-barreled shotgun?"

"Yes, sir." The brother searched about his pants looking for tobacco, or maybe just to keep his fingers busy.

"What did you give him?" The questions continued.

"I fed him, but I didn't have nothing to spare." The man slapped the table, aggravated that the only thing in his pocket was a ten-penny nail.

"Ammunition?"

"Five shells." The man said it indignantly, as if he should have owned more than those. "It's all I had would fit his gun. He said he'd shoot some turkeys and bring his game back."

"Where did the gun come from?"

Willard's brother scratched the back of his neck, thinking over this tough problem. "He said a friend lent it to him. Didn't say who it was."

"All right. When did he leave here?" Duff asked.

"Right after he rode in as a matter of fact," the brother said with relief. "We had some booger coffee then he left."

"Where did he go?"

"All he said was he was going camping for a few days and planned to hunt turkeys. I was happy to see him leave. He wanted a drink. I think he had a head start on a bottle of cane leavings before he got here. He's bad that way. I didn't have anything here, and I told him so."

"We're going to find him," Duff promised, "And if what you've told me turns out to be a lie that'll tie you right in with him. And you'd be up for murder, too."

The brother didn't blink at that. Innocent as a lamb.

"I reckon we'll camp outside for the rest of the night," Duff told him, "just in case Charley comes back."

"Help yourself," the brother said. "There's a pump outside, and the water's not too bad once you get used to it. My corral's not going to hold all your horses."

I watched the shadows of the girl getting dressed.

"That don't matter," Duff said. "We won't trouble you any more tonight."

The man was suddenly friendly now that it seemed he wasn't going to be beaten or taken away.

"My daughter would fix you some grub," he said, "but all we have is dried corn grits and not much of that. It might have a few weevils."

"We brung our own," Duff told him. He looked around the cabin. "I guess we can leave you a little of ours if you need it."

The men built their fires outside. Some quickly emptied the tins of boiled meat Duff had distributed and fell out, tired from the long day and night. The others stayed up, talking quietly around the flames. Duff kindled his own, and after seeing to our horses I joined him. The Captain shuffled around to make room for another body.

"Get here in the smoke," he said. "Keeps them mosquitos away."

"Won't all this commotion spook Willard?" I asked.

"Charley Willard? By this time he's sure to know we're after him. He won't be back here this night unless he wants to turn himself in."

"That would sure save us some trouble."

"Ain't likely to happen, though. I reckon Willard is a tough young bird, and he thinks he can outrun and outsmart the rest of us. And he may be right."

"No, we'll catch him," I said. I was never one to doubt myself.

"You're a confident feller, ain't you?" Duff laughed. "You ever fire that cannon you're packing?"

"I can sure knock the rattles off a rattlesnake, I guess."

"But you ain't never drawed down on a man, have you?

"No, of course not."

"I was hoping I was right about that. You're a little young to be shooting people."

"Maybe I ain't. My pa was younger than me when he enlisted."

Duff did some calculations. "I guess that could be true," he admitted. "I wasn't much older than you myself back in 1862 when I went in, so I see your point. We forget all about those details."

"What made you join up?" I asked, truly curious about the War. Not just because it had taken my father but because the stories they told made it all seem so ruthlessly bloody, but also heroic. Those Knights of the Round Table circled around my head, but these knights, like Captain Duff and Sheriff Sandy, were real and still walking around.

Duff found his pipe and packed it with the tobacco he had denied to Willard's brother. "Everybody joined up back then, Gawain. There was no way not to. Whoo-wee," he crowed. "I was ready for it, too! I met Sheriff Sandy and your dad in the cavalry. We all fought together, over and over, over and over....And over." He ran down. "Hell, our pants rotted out," he said, remembering.

"I wish I'd been there."

"A lot who was there wished they wasn't, or they had their life taken away far too early."

"I guess you killed a lot of Yankees."

Duff got his pipe lit and puffed. "Yes, I did," he said. "You've got to finish the job as best you can."

"The sheriff said the War killed my pa."

"That could be. Did you ever hear about your father at the Battle of Chickamauga?"

I had, more than once, but I shook my head and Duff continued.

"Well I was there. I didn't know your father as well as Sheriff Watson did, but I know he was a brave man because I saw him charge straight into a Yankee gun emplacement. The guns were protected by Yankee cavalry on both flanks and those boys had Spencers, so the air was just full of lead. Your pa got right up to them before he was shot down from his horse. The rest of us nonetheless took heart from his example and rode right into them guns, and we swept over them, firing our pistols and swinging our sabers right and left at those poor Yankee artillerymen. We said we won. It was near a place called Jay's Mill. So I do know your dad was a brave man. It was a stupid war though, son. You ought to be glad you missed it."

"I just wish I'd gotten to know him."

"Your father? Yeah, that's rough. You made out okay though, getting raised by Sheriff Watson."

"People say I look like him."

"Look like…?"

"The sheriff."

Duff shrugged. "Could be," he said.

"I never knew my mother either."

"I did. She was a real nice lady. And pretty."

"The sheriff said he was sweet on her but she married my pa anyhow."

"Is that what he said? Well, there you have it." There was more to that story than Duff cared to talk about. After a moment he continued, "I never knew my mother either. I felt sorry for myself when I was a little boy, but you get over them things."

I was very determined to learn what I could from Captain Duff. The chief deputy had the rugged, whiskery look and manly bearing that any young spirit would want to be around, and he was easy to talk to. I planned to stick close and pick up all the ideas and knowledge I could.

Since Duff was still smoking his pipe, I posed a question. "Why do you think Charley Willard killed Postmaster Abbe?"

"Hell, they've been killing people all over this country for as long as I've lived here," Duff said. "I heard about one just last week over by the Crews and Collier sawmill. They say some fellow named Durfee murdered Nelson Locklear. They caught the boy and chained him to a tree by his neck and supposedly somebody in the bushes shot him to death. Nobody has said boo about that."

"But what did Postmaster Abbe ever do to anyone?"

Duff thought it over. "Something personal between him and Willard, possibly," he suggested. "But from what I'm hearing it had to do with politics."

"Because Mister Abbe was a Yankee?"

"It might be. Cleveland getting' elected gave backbone to a whole world of cracker idiots here in Florida. I say that having always voted Democrat myself. But keep that to yourself, son. Most of the men on this posse are Republicans, to hear them talk. These are dangerous times to be speaking about politics. You ever read the Bible, Gawain?"

The change of topics disconcerted me, and I had to admit that my exposure to the Bible was limited. I'd never been required to study it even though the Ephrams were church people.

"I suppose not," Duff said. "I guess the sheriff's fine wife left you alone, didn't she? 'Course the poor woman, rest her soul, had five of her own to deal with. No proper church upbringing for you, was there Gawain? But you ought to give the Good Book a try. As you go on with your life, son, you'll find that people kill . . . they kill each other for lots of reasons." He turned serious. "Greed, land, politics, money. Good God, they kill!" Duff spat into the fire. "They don't always get punished for their wickedness in this world," he said softly, "but in the end the Lord sorts 'em all out."

I didn't know what to say to that, so I just poked at the fire. I had never warmed up to God, at least not the God that I could hear the preachers shout about inside their churches. And I had heard plenty of that, just standing outside in the churchyard and listening out of curiosity. I was concerned when the Captain pulled a worn black Bible from somewhere in his jacket and began thumbing through, searching for a page he had marked.

Duff noticed me and laughed. "Don't worry about it, Gawain. I like to read the Good Book because it gives me a peaceful feeling. And it helps get me to sleep. You've got plenty of years ahead, but this is a book I'd recommend."

I told him thanks but that I had another book to read first, meaning

Robert Burns. But then my tired eyes closed and I slouched down and fell asleep.

Clarinda Barlow had her dreams, too. She wasn't always going to have a life like this, slopping the hogs and swatting mosquitos out in the uncharted backwoods. She didn't mind the farming, and she loved her "Pa," but she hoped her destiny was better than that.

Her father never took her to town, any town, and he rarely went to one himself. It was almost like he was wanted by the law, but he insisted that he just "had no use" for all those other people and their rules, their "Keep Out" signs, and their fences. It was like a religious thing. If he had enough bearskins or hides from the old range cows he captured he would, of course, take them to Ft. Ogden to sell for hard currency. There were some things you needed cash money for, like pots, pans and gun shells. Other than that, they could raise what they needed, he said, and could rely on the drummers who passed through for the rest.

One of the drummers who rolled up to their cabin peddling cookware, shoes, fabric and canned food, also had some fancy books for sale that contained colorful drawings of animals. Clarinda was particularly taken with the book about birds, and she set about trying to trade for it. The peddler wasn't interested in the sack of potatoes she offered, but he did say he'd swap for a home cooked meal. He gave her a big smile and she smiled back. He was a fine looking man, with a high forehead and a pile of black hair, though he was old compared to her.

Under her father's watchful eye she prepared a simple dinner of salted ham, cornbread and collards from the garden, She blushed with pleasure when their guest declared that it was just about the best food he had ever eaten.

Afterwards, he said he need to go outside and check on his wagon. He gave a wink at Pa, which was enough to draw the old man along for a few pulls on the bottle. Clarinda cleaned up from dinner. After about half an hour her father came back in and said he needed to rest for just a few minutes. She knew he would probably be out for the night.

Wondering what had become of the drummer, Clarinda slipped out the door. She found him sitting on his wagon seat softly strumming a guitar. The music was transfixing though later she couldn't remember what song he was playing. He beckoned her to join him, and she climbed up beside him. Being next to a man in the dark was just about the most thrilling thing she had ever done.

He crooned for a while, smiling at her as he sang, and then offered to show her how. He wrapped his arm around her to place her hand on the frets and somehow she ended up kissing him. His hand found her breast, and she thought she would pass out from the rush of blood to her head. But she recovered quickly and shoved him away hard.

"I've got better sense than that, mister whatever-your-name is," she cried. "I'm saving my titties for a man with some real property, not just some old wagon!"

She jumped down. "And I'm keeping that book," she told him and stomped back into the house.

Songbirds and woods birds had always attracted her, but they had blended in with the rest of the scenery around the cabin. In the pages of her new book, the lavish and colorful drawings of birds left her spellbound. And, because of the circumstances of her acquiring it and its picture, she came to associate birds with the strange stirring between her legs.

CHAPTER EIGHT

A PLEASANT DAY ON A KILLER'S TRAIL

The morning came on cool and crisp. After a quick cup of coffee and a splash of cold water our posse rode on, going deeper into wild countryside where the roads were worse and the people fewer. I happened to fall in next to Piney Reasoner. I had heard of him before because he had been travelling around to the farms peddling seeds, demonstrating grafting techniques, and selling his own services budding trees. Farmers would pay as much as a nickel a bud for him to graft new varieties onto their old growth which had stout roots but piddling fruit. Piney wasn't much older than me, but he was already building a good business for himself. By his accent he was clearly a Yankee.

I asked him how he got into plants, and he told me part of his story.

"It's my family's trade, up in Indiana," he said. "I'm the first one to bring it here to Florida. I don't mean to brag, but I've got forty acres cleared in Orange Ridge. It's a nice grove of Genoa Lemon Trees and Mediterranean Sweet Orange. They're top of the line. My father is convinced now that this is the place where the future is, so he's followed me down and bought a big oak hammock which we're calling Oneco since we're the one and only company there."

I was naturally impressed by that and asked him what had made him come to Florida in the first place.

"I was living with my folks when I read a wonderful book about Florida," Piney explained with enthusiasm. "Have you ever read Sidney Lanier?"

"I guess not," I had to admit.

"I can recite it from memory." Piney's eyes turned dreamy and he stared up at the canopy of palms shielding us from the sun. "'To the tourist and sportsman desiring a mild flavor of adventure, this portion of Florida offers a charming field; and any invalid who is able to endure the comparative rudeness of this manner of life cannot but find benefit from the liberal air and genial appetites which range together along these quiet shores.'" Piney laughed and said, "Of course, I'm not exactly an invalid."

"And Manatee County ain't exactly mild and quiet," I had to point out.

"That's very true. But that book got my attention at home in Indiana, and here I am."

"Can you identify that bush over there?" I asked. It was a test.

"Maybe fetterbush?" Reasoner guessed. "And over there is a bunch of pawpaw."

So we passed the time. Was it pawpaw or polecat bush? What's gallberry look like? He pointed to a cup-shaped lily with red petals and a long yellow stamen and told me it was a Catesby's Lilly, named for a

British "naturalist." That's the first time I'd heard that there was a word for people who liked nature.

I noticed Captain Duff listening in on our conversation. I saw him smile and reach for the twist of North Carolina burley jammed next to a clasp knife in his vest. He said something to himself, and I think it was, "Ah, naturalists, are they? Armed to the teeth as Mexican gunslingers."

PLINY REASONER'S STORY

My name is actually Pliny, not "Piney," but around here there are very few students of history. My family is educated, maybe too much so. They named me for the Roman Admiral and naturalist who was famous for saying that "fortune favors the brave" before being smothered by the ashes spewing from Mount Vesuvius. And they named my younger brother Egbert after a king a thousand years ago from whom, I am told, Queen Victoria has descended. Very few of the settlers here in Sarasota can pronounce either name, but they can say Reasoner. My family indulged me and allowed me to follow my brave ancestor's advice and travel alone to Florida when I was seventeen. I haven't left since and don't aim to, but hope to meet a better end than my namesake.

In a little more than two years I have succeeded in clearing forty acres of pine forest and planting, for my nursery, peach trees, pear trees, several varieties of lemons, tangerines, satsumas, double pink geraniums, white oleander, cactus, Calla Lilies, apple trees, a Japanese plum, Key West gooseberries, tamarinds, pomegranates, magnolia trees, grape vines, figs, limes, guava trees, avocados, mangoes, sapodilla, papaya, a number of palms, and, for my table, sweet potatoes, cabbages, pumpkin vines, melons, strawberries, tomatoes and onions.

I admire the few men around here who have industry and good sense, and that included Charles Abbe. He was a progressive thinker and a talented farmer. We shared a love for citrus, experimental plants, modern agricultural techniques, and botanical research. He didn't exactly adopt me, but he shared my passions. He was, like my family, Republican, and devoted to fair play and the individual's right to reach for the stars – unlike the close-minded, Negro-hating, crowd I see calling themselves Democrats. They tried to lure wild hogs into my nursery to trample me out. They can never abide a bright man like me, or Mr. Abbe. With me, they have failed. Mr. Abbe, they killed.

There are other yahoos flocking to Florida, seeing it as their gold mine. They don't see the mountain; all they see is the gold. What I mean is, they don't want to expand upon the beauty and bounty of a virgin land, they just want to rape it and vanish.

Here's an example. I had a chance to join in on a sail to Key West with some Palma Sola friends who had purchased a vessel named The Permit. They were as fascinated with rare seashells as I was and with gathering exotic plants and seeds. The coast we hung to, heading south from Sarasota, is all mangroves, covering thousands of unchartered islands untouched by white people - though once, and maybe still, populated by Indians who prefer a lifestyle intricately and intimately involved with the natural world.

Punta Rassa, where the Caloosahatchee enters the Gulf, was, we thought, the last point of civilization before the beginning of the wildness of endless mangrove pirate coves, boundless skies of birds, and silvery flashes of fish in the wind's wake of our craft. But soon after passing the confluence, sailing south from Sanibel Beach, we passed by a spot along the low and desolate shore – the very weirdness and monotony of the scraggy vegetation is appalling – which has been given the name "Naples." Ah, it was the Bay of Naples over which my Italian namesake sailed to his death-by-volcano, so of course I was interested in what this new place might be like. So were my hosts. We pulled close to land, and what did I see? The most gigantic of humbugs! There were hundreds of white stakes marking 'avenues' and 'lots', destined, no doubt, to be gravestones to many a poor man's hopes – some fantastic development for Yankees with money to throw away for a bit of Florida and a whim. And NAPLES DOESN'T EVEN HAVE A HARBOR! How will the deluded lot-buyers ship their produce and fruit? They won't be able to make any living there whatsoever. I lost all interest in the place, and so did the crew, and on we sailed.

News travels faster than horses, and I'm sure that Charley Willard knew that the sheriff's posse was on his heels. Due to good fortune and Captain Duff's ability to read the tracks of horse and man - since by now we would pass spots where Willard had walked his horse – we were able to follow his circuitous route. And we noted that one of his boots had lost its heel. By accident or design the fugitive made somewhat of a roundabout and brought us to the farm of a man Captain Duff knew, William Bartholomew, the local Justice of the Peace. He might cut a good figure in court, but in his barnyard stacking firewood he looked just like any other dirt farmer in faded overalls.

His first lie was to say that he'd never heard of anyone named Charley Willard. His second lie was to say that he hadn't had any visitors for days.

I pointed to the sand by his barn door where there were obvious horse shoe prints and impressions of a man's shoe minus its heel.

Captain Duff stared hard at Bartholomew and spat a copious stream of tobacco juice at the ground between the lawyer's feet.

"You might want to work on that story 'cause Justice of the Peace or not, I'll handcuff you to that barn door until you tell me the truth."

Reluctantly, Bartholomew acknowledged the visit but spouted out another lie. He claimed he didn't know about any murder, at least not one in Sarasota.

Much later it came out, to my satisfaction at least, that Bartholomew was one of the gang that plotted the killings.

"You're a lawyer, a Justice of the Peace, and an officer of the court!" Duff roared, struck with the improbability of the man's statement. "Sworn to uphold the laws of the County and the State!"

"I don't have a thing to tell you," Bartholomew insisted.

We left it like that and rode on. I asked the Captain if he really would have cuffed the man to his barn, and he replied that, "A better idea would have been to shoot his pecker off! A lying lawyer is lower than the horse shit on my boots!"

From the branch of a laurel tree by the trail, Furman Whitaker retrieved a piece of worn fabric. The sleeve of Willard's shirt had torn off, and Furman twirled it in the air. "He's falling apart!" he cried triumphantly.

We camped another night on the trail, and ate canned beans and the last of a hard sausage.

CHAPTER NINE

THE CATASTROPHE

By the next day our posse was getting tired. We were covering a sandy path through sawgrass prairie, patches of saw palmetto, jungles of nettles, and sometimes a hidden prickly pear cactus. Everything that was alive and growing, it seemed to weary travelers, was pointed and tooth-like. The unwelcoming waist-high undergrowth spread as far as the eye could see baked by the burning glare of a pearly white sun. Even the ground radiated enough warmth to bother the horses.

The path we took was more suited to wild hogs than to human travelers or horses. To say we were a sorry lot would be an understatement. We weren't even sure of where our trail went – only that it was generally taking us south. The only motivation for us was imagining that Charley Willard must be feeling worse than we were. He had the curse of killing a man, and he was running out of Florida to hide in. Willard had to know that he was facing the hangman's rope when we caught him. Even worse for him, he was a drinking man without a drink. On a tired horse. Carrying a shotgun but only a couple of shells. Unless that rat Bartholomew had given him more.

We came upon a wide brown creek shrouded by crooked oaks, and the horses were excited. A mockingbird serenaded us from a tall pine and in the clouds a pink spoonbill showed off the feathers that the Florida plumers loved to pluck. Just as Duff pointed skyward at the rare and startling burst of color we were surprised, and in turn we surprised Charley Willard. He was crouched on the other bank not twenty feet away filling a canteen. Duff was the first to see him and reached for his gun. He yelled something unintelligible. Willard shouldered his own shotgun and fired. It blasted twice, emptying both barrels, one of which caught Duff high on the chest. The other load shattered the branch above his head.

The horses reared. "God Damn! Sorry sonofabitch got me!" Duff bellowed as he pitched off his horse and landed with a thud, his feet in the creek. The riders were stunned by the unhorsing of their leader, but Willard had more presence of mind. He jumped onto his horse and kicked it into motion. He disappeared into the trees on the far side.

Our posse was in disarray. I jumped from Whistler and fell over Duff, whose boots were thrashing the water, to protect him. Piney and Furman did something helpful, pulling clothes from their packs for bandages, but the others took cover behind the twisted oaks, prepared, perhaps, to fend off another attack.

"Sweet Jesus!" Duff shouted. "Don't worry about me! Go after him!"

Reluctantly, the blacksmith waded across the creek and peered into the bushes on the other side. Seeing nothing he returned to the horses, and then all of them splashed over into the brush in belated pursuit for the killer.

I couldn't leave. I cradled Duff's head.

"Good God, that hurts," he whispered. His piercing eyes blazed as if burning holes in the leaves overhead. "Take my Bible, boy," the old soldier told me through clenched teeth. "It's given me a lot of help in tough times." Blood from his chest covered his shirt, and a red trickle came from his nose. "Your father is…," he began.

"My father is what?" I cried.

"Well Hell," Duff said. He closed his eyes. "Just take me across the river and lay me in the shade of the trees," he murmured. "Or something like that."

He kept breathing but was drifting in and out of consciousness. It was obvious he was in a lot of pain. This being the first shooting I had had ever witnessed and the first gunshot-wounded person I had ever seen, I was quite distressed, fingers covered with the Captain's blood and his head on my lap. I got to my feet, shaking, trying to figure out what I could do to help him.

Suddenly the riders came splashing back across the creek.

"He's gone! Flyin' out of here like he's running from his maker. How's the Captain?"

They could all see he was in bad shape.

"Guess we better take him back to Manatee to his folks, and fast," the blacksmith said.

"Anyway, Willard will starve to death before too long," one of the men reasoned. He guided his horse over to Duff's mount, who was grazing leaves off a tree, and gently took the reins. "We have to take this man to a doctor, or to his next of kin," he said.

Piney Reasoner had a canvas ground cloth stowed behind his saddle and we quickly cut two saplings, tied the ground cloth to them and formed a rudimentary stretcher. He and Whitaker tied the stretcher to the Captain's horse and gently laid his body in it.

"I ain't dead," Duff protested loudly. He almost sounded surprised. Then he passed out.

"Mighty sorry end to this whole affair," Piney complained. "One good man dead, one bleeding out, and the killer still on the loose."

"Well let's go get him!" I protested. "Doesn't take all of you to ride one wounded man home."

The others looked dismayed to hear such a wild idea. They were all fatigued and unnerved by the swiftness with which Duff had been taken out and by all the blood on the ground. Besides, none of them had signed up to be a professional lawman.

"Like I said, Willard'll starve before long," the surveyor said. "He's got nowhere to go but south, down to the Peace River. Even if he gets across, which ain't easy, there's nothing but impassable county on the other side. You've got the Everglades in one direction and Ten Thousand Islands in the other and Seminoles in between. The sun and the damn mosquitos will drain him, brother. So let's ride poor Captain Duff back to civilization."

I agreed with part of that. "Sure, someone needs to ride the Captain back to his people, right now! But Willard is holed up in these woods. We can catch him!"

My objections were unavailing. Our posse, exhausted and depressed, and with a chief who urgently needed a doctor, finally and unanimously voted to return to Sarasota with their injured leader.

But not me. I was going ahead. And I was angry.

I went through the Captain's saddlebags and retrieved his Bible. Daring anyone to stop me, I transferred it to a pouch on Whistler's back.

In fairness I was younger and dumber than the others. Most had families, which I didn't. They were kind enough to take up a collection and leave me with two sacks of corn meal, some rich-smelling bacon, a spare canteen and five tins of smoked oysters. Whitaker had a .45 pistol, same caliber as mine, and he left me with an extra box of bullets.

I also took it upon myself to relieve Captain Duff of his Deputy Sheriff badge and the official arrest warrant in his vest. Both were stained with blood.

I was totally disgusted watching the men ride off. And a little lonely. But like the Captain said, you're supposed to finish the job. I pinned the badge on, inside my collar like the Captain had worn it, rather than on the pocket of my shirt. You could show it when that became necessary. Counting the extra box of bullets, Duff's Bible, my book of verse, the donated food, and assorted satchels, pots, ropes and tools it was getting crowded in my saddlebags and all around. I might have wished that Sheriff Watson were with me, or even Reuben Ephram to keep me company. But I had charted my course and was determined to see where it went.

I calculated that this was New Year's Eve, and it was a hell of a way to spend it. I had certainly seen more than enough fireworks, and I hoped the New Year wouldn't be any worse.

That night I slept near the creek's slow-flowing waters, without any fire or supper. I was tired as a worn out shoe. Whistler was my watch dog.

CHAPTER TEN

THE NEW YEAR

Morning came up fresh and bright on New Year's Day, and as the story was told to me, Alfred Bidwell walked the half-mile from his stately Sarasota house, still under construction, to his store on the bluff at water's edge. He wanted to verify that no damage had been done by any late-night carousers. Finding everything in order he locked the shop back up and strolled home along the neighborhood's sandy main street, called Cunliff Lane, named for the first family who built a house there. Bidwell's wife, Mary (though there was the hint of a scandal about the legality of their union), had bought their eighty acres from the State of Florida when they had moved from New York, and the Bidwells were in the middle of building their quite impressive home. Most of it was completed now, and habitable, and it was the shopkeeper's plan for the holiday to avoid any meddlesome chores in order to attend to his attractive flower garden of roses and white petunias, with a border of azaleas; all in need of a severe pruning.

As it was a holiday, he had celebrated by taking a nip from his own little medicine bottle, a tiny shot of morphine. He kept it in a locked metal chest at the store. The air this morning was breezy and cool, even nicer in the shade of the lane. As nice as could be. Hallucinating slightly from his drug of choice, Bidwell breathed in pleasurably both the beach air and the familiar sights of his town. He passed neighboring homesteads, the Alfords' house, and the Greers'.

Now his friend from Georgia, Jason Alford, was a good man, but strange. Gruff and belligerent to hear him talk, but he shied away from the real action. And Robert Greer, he was part of the Abbe crowd. Best to steer clear of him. Greer was on the list, and his day of reckoning would come. But in the meantime, be nice. Bidwell smiled. He had plans for the entire neighborhood.

Bidwell came upon Mr. and Mrs. Peter Crocker also on a stroll. He bade them a good morning, but they hurried past him, not eager to talk. That was their business Bidwell decided; probably they were friends of the Abbes'. People were starting to whisper about who was responsible for the postmaster's murder. They were just not the same since the postmaster's removal.

But this day was too pretty to worry about petty gossips.

Back at his house from his walk, Bidwell tarried outside among the flowers in the privacy of his back yard. He found clippers. With them in hand he stripped down to his sleeveless white undershirt. And then Ed Bacon showed up.

Bacon had come awake that morning with torn jeans and a serious hangover, cramped in a wooden porch rocker at his daddy's house two miles down the beach. The walls of the cottage were picturesquely sided with palmetto fronds, matching the thatch of the roof. Waddy, his father, and several of his brothers were all passed out inside, not inclined, it seemed, to strike out on this particular morning into the bay shallows for the oyster beds where the Bacons harvested their living - so Ed had the day to himself. Stumbling down the steps and into the yard, his head spun around dizzily. His family dwelling seemed to float by. Righting himself, he decided that the morning would be well spent finding a drink.

By the time he reached the Bidwell house in town Ed Bacon's head had stopped its pounding, and his feet has stopped their wayward diversions into the ditches. He was able to feel his tongue again.

The grocer, he saw, was playing among his flowers. Something a fairy would do, Bacon thought to himself, but since he owed so much money at Bidwell's store he knew better than to say anything like that. Bidwell was an important man, and Ed had lots of respect for how a big man could mess you up or help you out.

"Mornin' squire," he called loudly. Bidwell straightened up amidst the bushes where he had been enjoying his work, and he urgently waved Bacon into the garden.

"It may not be a good idea for you to be here, Ed," he whispered. "Some people are starting to talk."

"What are they talking about?" Bacon asked loudly, as he stepped with exaggerated carefulness between the beds of rose bushes. "They ain't been talking to me."

Some of the sweet sensations of the morning were dissipating in Bidwell's brain, and his angry streak was coming out.

"It's time to be intelligent and shut up about all this stuff," he snapped. "You know what I mean. They took Joe Anderson to jail, and he might be talking. No telling what Charley Willard will say if they ever catch him."

Contradicting the menace in his voice, Bidwell looked happy and cheerful as a blue bird, and while he spoke, his red-rimmed eyes opened wider and became ever more warm and inviting. This confusing aspect of the storekeeper's character always disconcerted Bacon, whose own manners were far more direct, but not necessarily scarier.

"Joe Anderson's your friend, not mine," Bacon grumbled. "You must be the judge of his trustworthiness. But Charley Willard wouldn't spill the beans to save his own ass, or his mother's ass, or any goddam ass, and you can quit worrying about him."

"Who said I was worried, Ed?" Bidwell patted his confederate's shoulder. "I ain't worried. Not one bit. Have you got your little boat all cleaned up?"

"Of course I do. Do you think I'm stupid?" Bacon was indignant.

"Of course not!" Bidwell exclaimed, but he did, in fact, think that Ed Bacon was dumber than a fence post. Bacon was good for only one thing and that was violent behavior upon the slightest provocation, and the murders of Tip Riley and Charles Abbe had been right up his alley.

Bidwell's own motivations were more complicated and sophisticated.

Postmaster Abbe had been poking into his real estate affairs and worse, poking into the legitimacy of his marriage to his darling Mary, who at that moment was looking out the curtains of their house to inspect this lounger who had invaded her gardens. It was not a sight she would approve.

"Look," Bidwell said to cut short this conversation, "we've got to maintain our discipline. Discipline above everything. You get on home and be about your normal business, and I'll do the same. Everybody from Bee Ridge will hold strong until this blows over. Then we will all reap the rewards. You understand?"

"Why sure," Ed Bacon said, putting on the stupid-grin face that he used when his mother caught him doing something wrong, "but ain't that payoff gonna be soon?"

"Soon enough!" Bidwell shouted before he got control of himself. He became confidential. "We're gonna make big money here," he said softly. "Big money. Hear me?" He was whispering now. "But this ain't about money, is it? It's about who owns this land, this country. It belongs to men like you, Ed Bacon. Men like you. You don't want to lose your birthright do you? Right?"

Ed shook his head.

"No, you do not want to lose your birthright. Florida, this God-blessed land, belongs to you and me, Ed. I'm going to get my share. Why not? And I'm going to make sure you get your share, Ed. And your family will prosper."

Bacon was impressed. He didn't care about his family, but nevertheless.

Bidwell was agitated despite his smile and longed to revisit his little brown bottle.

"I'd like to get back one of those jugs of moonshine I sold you," Bacon told the storekeeper.

"I already paid you for those, Ed," Bidwell explained politely. "They're at the store. I've already promised them to someone else."

Bacon's face grew hot and his cheeks red. "Well, I want a drink!" Now he was yelling, and Bidwell was alarmed.

"Well, since you put it that way," the storekeeper said soothingly, "I think I can fix you up. Being it's New Years, I believe I might have something you would like right out here in the spring house."

Casting a quick look back at the window, Bidwell led his visitor into the bushes behind the garden where, from the refreshing cool of the little well, he produced a half-full pint of yellow-clouded spirits.

"Take it and drink it in good health, Ed." Bidwell patted his back again. "And don't forget. This is all about discipline."

Bacon unscrewed the top and took a pull. "Fuck 'em all," he said, and saluted the clouds. He tossed back another swallow and gave Bidwell a mock slug to the chin, causing the older man to flinch.

"I'm with you, soldier," Ed told him, and Bidwell's stomach seized up. To his relief, Ed Bacon marched away with dramatic steps.

Bidwell rubbed his forehead with both hands and spoke to his sainted dead brother whose spirit he felt was somewhere overhead in the gray tresses of Spanish moss. His damn Union brother, peerless and brave at Gettysburg and Spotsylvania. "I think you had better troops than mine," Alfred Bidwell muttered. "And don't tell me how I'm supposed to act. This is Florida, not Buffalo, New York," he mumbled, warming up. "When people try to screw me, I fight with what's at hand. I do the best I can." The grocer dug into his pocket for his own little nip.

Next door, Bidwell's neighbor, Jason Alford, watched Bacon stumble out to the street. He withdrew into his yard praying that Bacon would not see him and, more importantly, knew how to keep his mouth shut.

JASON ALFORD'S STORY

They say I started the vigilante club, and I guess that's partly true. I was a Klansman for a bit back where I came from, but I never had a heart for the violent stuff. I was raised a Georgia Democrat, but no one can say I hate Yankees. I married one. I just don't intend to be pushed around by the rich Republican crowd who run everything around here. I made my own way, bought my own land from the state of Florida out on Bee Ridge.

I've survived misfortune. My house burned down, for God's sake, and my wife was killed in the blaze. I kept the farm but had to move my family to town. That's six kids, Eva, Dicey and the four boys. We packed into a little house I could afford. Times were rocky for quite some time, don't you know. People said I was a cow thief. Sheriff Watson said so, but his bull was a stray when I found it. And then they accused me of stealing another cow and got me arrested. The second time around I had some better friends to back me up.

See, not long after I moved the kids to town, I met and married my second love, a young widow woman who happened to own a nice big house right behind Alfred Bidwell's store. Her husband was buried in the back yard. He was a Union cavalry officer, so don't say that I hate Yankees. When I was charged for theft that second time, Bidwell, Dr. Leonard Andrews, and my neighbor Joe Anderson, all fine people, went my bail. Naturally I was acquitted, but not until I travelled overnight twice to the courthouse in Pine Level.

I was angry about all the community's affairs after that, and me and other angry men arranged a meeting at my house. Dr. Andrews called us all together, but my new wife's big house was the best place for the most people. Seventeen turned up, and we chartered the Sara Sota Vigilance Society. It was a Democratic Club, a club to watch out for the morals around the county and to keep the land open for settlers like me. Putting it plain, there's some people around here it would be better if they got a good strapping and was run out of town.

Now, there are people who don't like me and my big mouth. When I'm riled up, I speak the truth and don't care who hears it. And I was heard saying that we need to tar and feather some of these miserable devils like

Postmaster Abbe. But talk's one thing. I never lifted my hand to kill no one.

I guess I did want Tip Riley dead. I saw him at the Pine Level Courthouse, when he was about to be let off for murdering his lady friend just because she was going to have his baby, a poor widow herself. Who can stand a man like that living in your community? And to be truthful, I suppose I did try to get old Joe Anderson and that no-account Charley Willard to show a little backbone and kill Postmaster Abbe. I'm afraid my daughter Eva, and my wife, of course, probably heard me going on about that. Like I said, I'm not known for having a quiet mouth.

Abbe was just a rich so-and-so who lorded over everybody that he owned damn near the entire bayfront in town, and then he was trying to get those squatters out in the country to assert land claims that would keep pioneers like me, who could actually make something of ourselves and our property, from acquiring any more acreage. It made sense to me that he should be got out of the way, and I guess people heard me say that, and it gave them the idea that I was the leader of something.

I was all for going after the lot of them, sure, but my wife, Elizabeth, talked me down. She got mad about it after the meeting at our house because she had heard some of what was being said. She reminded me that I had six mouths to feed, not counting her and me. On the other hand, a man has got to do what a man has got to do. I guess on account of her I did back off from the dirty work. My hands are clean as spring water. But I can tell you one thing.

If any trouble comes out of all this for me, I ain't waiting around to see what happens. I'll not be accused and put before that kangaroo court in Pine Level again. I'll be a man on the run.

Across the Florida scrub and by myself I followed a trail suitable for farm wagons, winding in slow curves across the prairie. I spied a few cows, but the sun was high in the sky when I got my first glimpse of another human being. A rude buckboard being pulled slowly by a large mule came in my direction. As it neared, I saw there were two people dressed in black on the seat. The driver cried "Whoa!" to stop his mule when they came alongside. He was a big fellow, sweating in the sun, with a broad face under a wide brimmed hat, probably about my age. His passenger, wrapped in a black coat, stared straight ahead.

"Howdy," I said. "Have you been on this road long?"

"About two days," the young man replied. He took out a red handkerchief from his trousers and wiped his forehead. "It's hotter than I expected after such a cool morning."

"Yeah it's unseasonable," I agreed. "I'm looking for a man named Charley Willard. He's wanted for murder."

"I haven't seen a soul," the youth said and tapped the reins to steady his mule.

There was something strange I thought about his passenger. She was a frail-looking woman, and she seemed remarkably pale. Her eyes didn't move. It was as if she wasn't even there. "Is that lady sick?" I inquired.

"She was. Now she's passed away. This is my mother, Ophelia. She died yesterday morning, on New Year's Eve. I'm taking her around to visit all of her favorite places before I lay her in the ground."

"But she's dead!" I protested.

"Isn't that what I just said!" he shouted at me angrily. "Is there something wrong with your ears?"

"Nothing wrong with my ears, or what's between them either. You ain't supposed to be riding around with a dead person, even if it is your mother."

"Who says?" the traveler demanded and looked quite haughty.

That stumped me. "Well, it just ain't right," I said.

"I'll thank you not to tell me what's right and wrong about my own mother," the fellow yelled, and he flicked his reins. The mule's large haunches rose and fell as the wagon lurched slowly forward.

"Stop!" I cried, but they didn't. I watched the wagon rattle on, getting smaller and smaller.

"Well, I'll be damned," I told Whistler. "I guess I ain't much of a lawman. Or maybe people do that all the time." From somewhere a laugh came out of me which I was helpless to stop. I must have hooted for a full minute before I could get control of my windpipes and wipe my eyes on my sleeve.

I gave Whistler a nudge and we resumed our journey, but I was still subject to sudden bouts of laughter for several miles down the road. Nerves, I guess.

It was mid-afternoon and I was quite tired from the boredom before I came upon a second party, two men riding toward me on a long wagon pulled by a team of horses. It was loaded down with sacks of lemons and baskets of melons which they were going to sell at a market in Osprey. They were friendly enough but didn't admit to seeing Willard or anyone else, and they rode on. I at least learned from them that the road I was on ran from a ford called Rocky Flats on the Myakka River to the new county seat at Pine Level twenty miles ahead. They warned me that Pine Level wasn't much of a town, but it was helpful to know where I was.

Just as I was speculating about whether there might be a store with food items in "not much of a town," my road crossed a small creek. As luck had it, I spied a narrow pathway splitting off and meandering with the creek southward. It would have been easy to miss, but, getting down from Whistler and studying the ground, I saw that the hoof prints I'd been following all day branched off that way. So I took the new path.

That sandy passage soon forked, and forked again, a maze of trails through the dry pine hammocks alternating with wet sloughs, flush with myrtle and laurel oaks, in which birds and more birds chattered chaotically. I was distracted from the tedium of the place, by plants I could identify, like hog plum with its clusters of yellow flowers and cutting thorns. I'd heard that the Indians made a bath from hog plum bark to sooth their sore muscles, and I thought I'd like some of that right about now. Thinking back, it was a good thing Willard didn't shoot me off my horse, since I had certainly stopped paying attention to the dangers of the hunt.

The sun went behind the trees early, though the sky kept its burnished golden glow, but I began thinking of a warm campfire.

Of a sudden, I smelled the smoke of a cook fire. That brought me up short, and I quickly dismounted and tied Whistler to a fragrant cedar by the trail. It had suddenly become cold. Slipping through the trees I spied a wilderness cabin. It was built of pine planks and palmetto roofing, the sort that's good for an overnight hunting trip. The cabin wasn't lit, but was illuminated by the rising moon, which came up full while I squatted on the ground watching with my tired horse well behind me. I saw a cow tied up under a lean-to. I made out what I took to be a big garden in the field behind the cabin, but it was mostly covered in winter weeds. And there was a horse, too, behind a fence by the lean-to. I didn't figure that Willard was in this place. It wasn't his horse in the corral. But just in case, I waited.

I ate one of my tins of oysters, but they didn't sit well with me. And the air got to be cold. Just like it usually is in January.

The only sound was the lonesome call of the Chuck Will's Widows in the trees above. The only light was the moon. Weird things started striking me as funny. What if I got eaten by a panther and no one but my horse would know it? Ha!

Though wiregrass makes a sorry place to sit your butt, I still grew sleepy. To stay awake, I fetched up my little book of poetry.

Flipping to a random page, I read, whispering the strange verses.

> *Ae fond kiss, and then we sever;*
> *Ae farewell, and then for ever!*
> *Deep in heart-wrung tears I'll pledge thee!*
> *Warring sighs and groans I'll wage thee!*
> *Who shall say that Fortune grieves him,*
> *While the star of hope she leaves him?*
> *Me, nae cheerful twinkle lights me;*
> *Dark despair around benights me.*

A hoot owl scared me, but I got back to it.

> *I'll ne'er blame my partial fancy,*
> *Naething could resist my Nancy;*
> *But to see her was to love her*
> *Love but her, and love for ever.*
> *Had we ne'er lov'd sae kindly,*
> *Had we na'er loved so blindly,*
> *Never met – or never parted,*
> *We had na'er been broken-hearted.*

It was dawn when I opened my eyes. Robert Burns had hit the ground. The cow, the horse, and the cabin were all still there, but a lantern now glowed through its only window. The first pink of sunlight was announced not by a rooster but by the cow, impatient to be milked.

In a few minutes the front door creaked opened and a female with a red blanket wrapped around her came outside and went to the pump. She filled the bucket and used a little of what was in it to splash her face. She carried the bucket inside and closed the door.

The situation called for some caution, but I was hungry as hell. Staying in the shadows, I made my way to the side of the house. Crude as it appeared, it was a house. There were sounds of a fire being stoked up inside and an iron pot grating against an iron stove. I was thinking breakfast.

That being paramount, I made a loud knock on the porch pole. This caused a considerable scuffle inside, with a woman yelling, "Pa!" and a loud snorting. The door wasn't latched so I pushed it open and said, "I ain't here to hurt nobody."

The female in the blanket had gotten dressed. She was young and her fingers covered her mouth. The one I was more worried about was an old fellow with a bull-like forehead and a pointed chin who came stumbling out of the corner.

"Who! What! You doin'?" The man groped for words.

"Sorry to surprise you, mister. I'm Gawain MacFarlane. I've been deputized by the sheriff to find a man name of Charley Willard. He's killed once that I know of. Have you seen him?"

The man looked offended but shook his head no, and the young girl gave me a blank stare.

"Has he been here?"

"No!" the girl declared loudly.

"Wouldn't have him here," said the man, fastening on his overalls.

"You know who I'm talking about?" I asked.

"Charley Willard. Yes, I know him," said the man.

"Then maybe you know he's wanted for murder. Any idea where he might be?"

"I wouldn't doubt he's capable of murder," the old man said, looking more confident now that his pants were secured, "but I couldn't guess where he is."

"In Hell, I hope!" stated the young woman coldly.

"Not a friend of yours?" I inquired.

She waved the hair off her forehead and gave me a glare. Clean her up and she'd be pretty, was my thought. "Did he bother you?"

But she turned to the stove and stirred whatever was in her pot.

"I ain't had a hot meal in a day or two," I pointed out.

Pioneer etiquette being what it was, they shared their breakfast with me, praise the Lord! Coffee made from something else, maybe yaupon, served in blue tin cups, and fried sweet potatoes and grits on blue tin plates. But to me it was steak and eggs.

I noticed that there were two beds in the cabin. "Y'all related, I suppose," I said, being conversational.

"My daughter, thank you," the old man told me. "I am Pa Barlow and my daughter here is Clarinda Barlow."

"My ma's died," the girl added, which I thought might not exactly be true since it drew a frown from her father.

"Sorry to hear that, Miss. Mine's gone, too." I took the moment to look more closely at our cook. I saw now a freckled face, blue eyes, and a shape that appealed to me. She was a little disheveled, which was to be expected living so far out of the world, but she was nowhere near as unwashed as her dad. Her blond hair was tied up in a bun, modestly I thought. My eyes were drawn to her bangs slipping out on both sides of her ears. Even if I hadn't been four days on a rugged trail, and hadn't seen my Captain laid low, I would have commented that she was very pretty. I was about to utter something brilliant when she took a bite off her fork and swallowed before saying, "I hope you catch him quick"

"I plan to," I assured her. "He near killed Captain Duff. He blew him right off the saddle. And he killed another important man in Sarasota. The postmaster."

We continued our meal in silence. When I finished I told them, "I'll be going. And thank you for the grub."

Pa Barlow showed me to the door, and put his arm around my shoulder. "Lots of land around here," he told me. "Lots of it cheap. We need neighbors."

I got my gear together and saw to my horse. The girl followed me outside, while her farther watched from the doorway.

"If Charley Willard shows up, he won't get nothing here," she assured me, while I hoisted the saddle onto Whistler's back. "What'd you say your name was?" she asked.

"My name is Gawain Wallace MacFarlane," I told her, though I rarely gave out my middle name.

"You're just about the only boy anywhere close to my age I've ever seen," she said. And I guess I was a good-looking young man with my shock of brown hair thrown across my forehead. I laugh at those pictures of me now.

"Is that right," I replied, being very cultured. "Well, I've seen lots of girls your age."

"Where do you live?" she asked me.

"Up near Manatee City, by Bradentown."

"Where's that?"

"It must be thirty miles from here, and the road's bad."

"I've been to Pine Level for church one time," she said. Her eyes and mine took in her surroundings. She knew her explorations had been limited.

"Weren't there any boys there?" I was teasing her.

"Might have been somewhere, but I didn't see 'em. We was invited by some preacher who came through here, but not very many people came. 'Course there ain't too many folks around here to begin with."

"I got to go." I stepped into the stirrup and swung my leg up over the saddle.

"You seem nice enough," she said, still interested in me.

I was confused by this, I must admit, but I said, "Thank you kindly," but I remember adding some very dumb words. "I don't know too much about what to say to girls." And I'm sure I blushed.

"That man you're looking for is dangerous as a mad dog," Clarinda warned me "There's nobody around here who's going to have any pity on him if he's caught." Her cheekbones and jaw were clinched tight when she said this. A very resolute young lady.

As I recall the gallantry of my youth, I arose to my full height on my horse and touched my hat in farewell.

CHAPTER ELEVEN

GETTING TIRED OF THE WHOLE THING, UNTIL...

Winter days were short and just poking along without seeing any sign of the man I was after, I began to wonder whether I was just wasting my time. I wished that someone were along to keep company, someone I could talk to other than my horse. I recalled fun days with Reuben.

A few months back he had introduced me to what he called "corn squeezins." Someone in the country showed him how to make a still out of an old zinc milk jug and some copper water pipe, and Reuben had gotten hold of enough supplies to undertake the project. It took him about a week, but when he had it all set up he took me to his hiding place to show it off.

The clunky pot was sitting on a grate above a smoldering fire.

"And it comes out here." He pointed to the clear liquor dripping into a Mason jar. "And you drink it like this." He produced a full bottle from a pile of leaves and took a swallow. His eyes bulged and his face got red.

"Now you try it," he wheezed.

I took a teaspoon full and my tongue lit up. "That tastes like tobacco spit," I coughed.

"But is has a better effect," Reuben assured me and drank again.

He passed the bottle back, and I took another pull. Then another. We finished a third of the bottle, got to feeling sick and staggered back across the pasture to find some water to drink at the barn. I was on my knees before we got halfway there.

When I got done puking, I resolved not ever to drink that stuff again – a resolution I forgot in coming years. But Reuben took it in a different direction. He began swiping whatever glass jars he could find, filling them up with shine, and hiding them in the barn. Then he went to work selling them. Naturally, he fell in with a new bunch, boys his own age or older, and he cultivated a tight band of moonshine peddlers who operated for an entire summer, until people began getting sick, and the location of the still started getting publicly known.

By then, Reuben's reputation had fallen into disrepair, and he and Mr. Ephram had words. The Ephrams were as respectable as church deacons, in fact they were church deacons, and they told Reuben to straighten up or get out. He chose to get out, but only as far as the barn, and he moved in with me.

This situation was unsatisfactory for several reasons, the main one being that I liked my privacy, but there had been no time to sort it out before I rode to the pig roast and ended up being summoned by the sheriff to go after the Abbe killers.

I was just considering how I might rearrange things with Rueben when I got back home, when I suddenly saw something: a clear hoof print in the dirt. I was almost positive that it had been made by Willard's horse. Now my blood was pumping!

I hastened along, and the path we were following eventually broadened. Whistler and I came upon the Peace River. Close to the water, hoof prints and animal tracks obscured each other on the muddy trail which descended down the riverbank to a ford. A rusty cable was bolted above the water to sturdy trees on both banks. On the far side, fifty yards away, there was a junky flat-boat ferry. I could see that it was made of raw timbers barely long and wide enough to accommodate, precariously, a wagon.

Not requiring such transport, I gave Whistler a nudge and rode him splashing across the stirrup-deep water, agitating clouds of bottom mud into the lazy current. An alligator was sunning itself on a small beach close to the ferry, but Whistler missed it, thank goodness.

On the other bank a number of old wagons with wooden wheels and steel rims sat abandoned in the weeds beside a fenced corral which contained one sad-faced mule. The worn-out animal looked like he'd been worked hard for many a long year and now had made himself part of the poverty-stricken scenery.

The headquarters of this operation was apparently a tin shack near the riverside which was sheltered behind a tall curtain of bamboo and oak trees. Some kind of decorations, statues of wild animals crafted from clay and shell, and assorted skulls and rib bones, were arranged around the yard. I sized the place up as a good spot for a criminal to hole up, so I unholstered my pistol and instead of knocking, kicked open the door and ducked inside. Nothing stirred, and it took me a moment to see through the dust floating in the shadows and perceive a gaunt man sleeping soundly on the only chair in the room. There was an empty brown bottle on the floor between his bare feet.

Feeling my unwelcome shake on his shoulder, the man started awake, focused on me and cursed.

"Christamighty!" he howled, stretching his face and working his jaw to get things operational.

"Afternoon," I said, politely as I could.

"Who are you?" he demanded. Sweat bees were buzzing around his head.

"Name's MacFarlane. I'm looking for a man."

"Who would that be?" The proprietor stretched and farted. "I see you're just a boy, but have you got any shine, snuff, smoke or chew you might want to part with?"

"Naw. I don't drink or partake. The man I'm after is Charley Willard. Know him?"

"I know some Willards over by Burnt Store, but I ain't heard of a Charley. What do you want him for?"

"For murder. He killed the postmaster up in Sarasota, and he may have killed a Manatee County sheriff's deputy."

"Whew! That's some killing." The scraggly man stroked his chin whiskers. "Don't know why I ain't heard about that. I get a lot of news here from people going across. We get right busy in the spring with people travelling to and from Fort Ogden, but it's quiet nowadays. Nobody said nothing about it to me." The man got to his feet and felt above the top of the wall for a pouch of tobacco and his clay pipe. "What's your interest in this Willard? Kin of yours?"

"No kin to me. I'm a Deputy Sheriff, and he's a wanted man."

"Sure enough?" The ferry keeper looked incredulous. "You don't much look like a sheriff."

"See this badge?" I displayed my pin. "And I guess you can see this gun, can't you? Now let's not waste time. What do you know?"

"I don't know nothin'. But I'll tell you what I did see, since you're asking." He found a match and struck it on the tin roof nailed close to his head. The flare briefly took some of the gloom off the hot, tiny cabin.

"What's that?" I prompted him.

"About a hundred paces that way," he pointed into the woods, "you'll see a fork in the road. The main one off to the right'll run you over Shell Creek to Trabue. The other one heads west over toward Liverpool. Take that one just a little ways and you may come across a dead horse. There was one there last night, but the buzzards and an alligator was fighting over it. It may be gone now. At any rate, no rotting corpse lasts long around here."

"Was it Willard's horse?"

"How the hell would I know? I don't even know this Willard you're going on about. Just a horse to me. And it was poorly treated."

I soon found what was left of the poor creature. Dried blood covered its gnawed bones and last strips of flesh. The buzzards were working it over good. Gruesome black birds, glaring at me, grudgingly strutted back a few feet into the palmettos while I inspected the remnants of loose skin surrounding the bones. It was a horse, and it could have been Willard's.

I took my whip and scattered the carrion-eaters. There weren't any human remains around as far as I could detect. The horse corpse had a shoe that looked like the one I was following. Then down the trail a bit I noticed human prints, a few impressions of a man's boot in the soft ground. The heel of one boot was missing and the other sole appeared to be wearing thin. In fact, I could make out three toes poking out of the leather.

Willard was half-barefoot!

I jumped back on Whistler, anxious to distance myself from the stench of dead horseflesh and catch up with a man who could not be far ahead. But this will show you how young I was then. Within five minutes I was distracted by a glimpse of a red snake coiled up in the sponginess of a wet spot atop a rotting stump. I did like snakes and had quite a collection! Fetching a string from my saddlebags I slipped off Whistler and walked slowly toward that slinky critter. It was a frightening bright red, with black and yellow rings behind its head and every few inches down its long body, a distance of perhaps two feet. I was excited because I thought it a venomous coral snake, which was missing from my zoo in the barn, but I was disappointed to see this was its non-poisonous cousin, a scarlet king snake.

Oh well, I didn't have one of those either. I dropped my little noose lower and lower, staring straight into its tiny pair of beady black eyeballs. My loop went over the snake's head and I jerked it hard. The serpent was caught!

I yanked the struggling reptile off the log and deposited it into a pouch on my saddle. My purpose for capturing the king snake was simply to carry it back home and put it in the fish tank I had acquired for such specimens. And for this, I had probably allowed Willard to get a mile further down the road.

Kicking myself I moved fast and crossed some country, son. Whistler and I came out of the trees onto a sawgrass prairie where the trail was so overgrown that I had to dismount and lead him in some places. Except for buzzing insects, the silence was pervasive. A startled piglet scurried across our path and back into cover, causing us both to jump. I was sweating in the heat and maybe dizzy. I imagined Willard behind every yucca and palmetto, crawling among the bugs. Next I imagined Clarinda waving me ahead. I recalled the little bit of Burns poetry I had memorized.

"Her yellow hair, beyond compare,
Comes tricklin' down her swan-like neck,
And her two eyes, like stars in skies,
Would keep a ship from a wreck."

Whistler and I finally reached a sprawling oak hammock the other side of the rugged plain when I was suddenly taken totally by surprise by a group of Indians resting in the shade. Their horses were grazing back in the trees, and two cows, maybe more, were tethered in the flat behind them, feeding on the tall grass.

I had a good idea what they were; Seminoles. I'd seen their kind before, a husband and wife who cleaned the hardware store and the bank in Manatee City. These men were dressed along the same lines – long tunics, torn and sweat stained, but colorful, cowboy hats, and worn leather leggings. Seated, they examined me, a stranger whose approach they had probably been observing for the past twenty minutes.

I tipped my hat hello.

A stocky man with a shell necklace, evidently the leader, was leisurely smoking a black cigar. He rose up and waved me forward. To show my good intentions I dismounted and walked into their little camp, holding Whistler's reins. According to the peace treaty these Indians were supposed to be in Oklahoma, I was sure of that, or on some reservation much further south where white men were non-existent. In any case they weren't supposed to be here. Another member of the band stood up slowly, as if to protect the chief. The others remained on the log, smoking.

"Nice cows," I said. "Look pretty fat. Yours I suppose."

"What about your horse?" the leader asked. "Whose is that?"

I flipped over my collar to show them the badge. "It's my horse," I said. "I'm looking for a man, might have passed through here last night or this morning. He's on foot."

"What is your business with him?" The Indian asking the question could have been almost any age, but he had the manner of a man considerably older than me. He didn't seem to be exactly awe-struck by my badge. He didn't seem to be belligerent either.

"He's a murderer, and I'm commissioned to catch him." I took a chance and squatted down. Without hesitating both Indians did the same.

"Want some smoke?" the older man asked.

"Naw. Wouldn't mind some water from that creek though, for me and my horse."

"It's all free. You can help yourself. We already ate or you could have some food."

"I'm not hungry," I told them, though I was. "Have you seen a tall man, a cracker, wide shoulders, a mustache, maybe worn out and nasty, probably on foot? No shoes?"

The Indian took a puff on his black cheroot and watched the smoke rise up and disappear into the still air. "He came through here," the man said finally. "Not much left of him. No toes. Skeeters eat him up. He's burned all red by the sun. Redder'n me." The men on the log all laughed.

"Did he have a double-barreled shotgun?" I asked.

"Like this one?" One of the seated Indians pulled the weapon from behind his log. I changed my opinion about who the chief was.

"That would be it."

The man placed the gun back on the ground behind him. I dismissed any idea of trying to take it.

"Glad to know he's unarmed. Where did he go?"

"He went off that way, into the 'Blackjack.'" The man motioned toward a distant line of trees across the next stretch of prairie.

"What's the Blackjack?" I was unfamiliar with such a thing.

"A place you don't want to be. No trees like it anywhere else. A hog can't even get through, its branches are so thorny. Legend says our people planted those trees hundreds of years ago. They used it as some kind of jail."

"Your people being Seminoles?"

"A lot older than those Seminoles, but you can call us whatever you like."

"Doesn't matter to me," I said. "Why did he go that way?"

The Indian shrugged.

"I mean, after he gave up his gun and all?"

"Must have seemed like his best bet, getting lost," the wrinkled man on the log piped up. "Probably he'll die in there."

I nodded like I understood, which I was beginning to. "I never heard of any Blackjack trees," I said.

"This is the only place they are," the Indian said. "At least I hope it is. You won't even see them in the Glades. Cows go in the Blackjack, forget about 'em. Not even dogs come out."

"But there's a man, a spiritual man, who lives in there," the important looking Indian on the log said. "You'll see him if you stay on the trail."

"You mean someone lives in those woods?" I asked. "Doing what?"

"He's a medicine man, I think, but not one of ours. He prays a lot. Maybe he's a Baptist."

"I don't care if he saves Willard as long as he don't feed him," I said. "I've about got him wore out the way I want him."

Another of the Indians on the log laughed quickly and stopped.

The speaker shrugged. "They say he eats people. Don't know if that's true, but we stay away from him."

"Well thanks for the tip," I said. I thought they were making up a story just to scare me. "Reckon I'll take a look." I climbed back on Whistler and gave the reins a tug. The band of Indians watched my departure in silence.

It took us half an hour to get to the Blackjack forest. As Whistler plodded slowly though the rugged scrub I kept looking right, left and back over my shoulder watching for a desperate outlaw and a flesh-eating preacher. At last we reached the edge of the fearsome woods; I found it to be an imposing twenty-foot tall barrier of thorny, crowded, desolate winter-time trees, like a thunderhead cloud had sunk to the earth, put down roots, and sprouted black swords. Where the green grasses of the prairie touched its well-defined edges, the blades of grass shriveled as if even their roots recoiled from the jungle of blistered trunks with their tangles of brittle branches.

"Never seen anything quite like this before," I said, breaking the silence. I didn't even hear any birds singing. Adding to the brooding strangeness, the shadows cast by these unusual trees were growing longer. It seemed like the day was only half over, but it would soon be dark.

The only reason I could imagine for Willard deciding to drag himself into this morass was that the Indians hadn't given him a choice. I sure as hell wasn't personally interested in entering it. It was gloomier and creepier than any place I'd ever dreamed of, let alone seen. All my doubts about undertaking this mission on my own came flooding back over me. Was anybody back home concerned about the success or failure of my journey? I could only speculate.

CHAPTER TWELVE

SPECULATION

Back in Sarasota the killing of Postmaster Abbe had cast a pall over the small town. He had been a public figure, known by everyone. He had been one of the largest landowners around. His family was joined by marriage with the Whitakers, Sarasota's pioneer family. People, most people, liked him.

The absence of a body made a funeral impossible and townsfolk all knew more than they wanted to about the circumstances of the crime. Its striking violence was a damper on their customary friendliness. The gunman, everyone knew who he was, had eluded capture, leaving the wound open, questions unanswered. Willard's fiancé left town, and neither his friends nor his enemies wanted to talk about the crime or the killer.

The men of the returning posse hurried through Sarasota on their way to Manatee City with the gravely wounded Captain Duff, but they were without Willard and without me. The fact that the murderer was still being hunted by a youngster named Gawain MacFarlane, the sheriff's foster son, was no comfort at all. It seemed a good bet that the murderer would dispatch me easily and be back in Sarasota in days if not hours to take his revenge on anyone who talked. The friends of Postmaster Abbe took extra precautions to secure their homes. In the whole town, everybody, even the women and some children, walked about armed.

At Abbe's store the riders quickly picked up fresh bandages and a bit of morphine for Duff's pain, but there was no doctor in the village so they kept going north to Manatee City where the Captain's family lived.

News of Duff's shooting hit Sheriff Watson hard. The prospect of losing his best friend within a year of losing his own wife sent him into a hole. Also he didn't let on, but I'd like to think he was mightily worried about what was going to happen to me, Gawain, out all by myself somewhere in the wilderness between the rivers. Maybe his conscience even bothered him for his years of inattentiveness to my welfare. I trust he vowed to take a greater interest in my future development, God preserve him. He's dead now, as I write this.

SANDY WATSON'S STORY

 What a sad way had Gawain come into the world.

And I had played a part in that, hadn't I? I can still see his crippled father, Major MacFarlane, bony fist gripped around that Colt .45, and pointing it straight at me. "You bastard!" Wallace MacFarlane cursed me, his boon companion since childhood; I ducked and felt the bullet pass over my head as I scrambled for the door. The damaged man threw the revolver after me and it hit me in the back. It might have been a blessing for all, short years later, when the house burned down, taking with it the maimed warrior, too sick and bitter to want to live. And his wife, the young mother, dying a few years earlier, while giving birth to Gawain, maybe that was a blessing, too, taking her guilt with her.

I've managed my own guilt the best way I know how, raising young Gawain and all, though some might say I could have done a better job of it. His life out on my farm with the Ephram family might not have been easy, but he always had plenty to eat and was kept safe. Hell, he was loved, by the Ephrams. I'd have had him in town with my other children, but the missus, well, she wouldn't stand for that given the circumstances of his birth, and all.

Yes, I've tried to lead an honest and upright life. But that is starting to be hard to do. This whole part of Florida is changing fast. Fortunes are going to be made from the land, the railroads, the oranges, and all of those rich

Northerners who have discovered the exhilaration of what they call roughing it, that is, reeling in tarpon and shooting alligators. And those other rich Northerners who have the capital to buy this paradise and chop it up into little bits and pieces. I have to wonder how I will fit into the future. I have carried a gun for many years, but the law is now being made by whoever owns the courthouse. Cold-eyed violent men, with money behind them have been set loose in the country. They are apt to kill any honest man who stands in their way, like they killed the postmaster. A fellow might need to adapt to survive, including the County Sheriff.

Against all odds, Captain Lemuel Duff managed to keep breathing. In fact, he came loudly awake. Under the care of his wife and daughters, and a real physician named Dr. Ruddy from Bradentown, Duff gasped his way back to alertness and announced that he was well enough to get out of bed. But the pain was undeniable and was addressed by narcotics dissolved in a cup of sweet iced tea, which carried him back to sleep. Two days later he awoke, famished, a problem his caretakers were only too happy to rectify

Drinking his chicken broth, I'm told that the Captain's first question was about me. When he learned that I had been left in the wilderness to search out Willard by myself, he became enraged and could only be soothed by his first-born, Suzanna, who laid cold compresses on his forehead and stroked his shoulders.

But not soothed for long. As soon as he could sit up and chew his own bread, he vowed to ride out and find his "ward." "What's Sandy doing for him?" he yelled.

Sheriff Watson came to visit on the day Duff became alert, and he was not surprised to hear the question. He replied that he had faith in my survival abilities, but he doubted that I would ever get anywhere close to Charley Willard, who was a Florida cracker to the core and would be able to elude my capture.

"But he could kill your boy!" Duff hollered, loudly enough to bring his wife to the door.

"I thought about that," the sheriff said. "How could I not think about that Lemuel? But I believe that rascal Willard is long gone from these parts. I've sent a message to the sheriff in Key West to be on the lookout for him. I'm fairly sure that's where that spawn of the Devil will turn up, if he survives in the swamps, which isn't likely. Gawain will ride back here safe and sound before long."

All Captain Duff could do was fume. Another day, and he was on his feet, though he shouldn't have been. While forty miles to the south, the county's youngest deputy was continuing to size up the "Blackjack."

CHAPTER THIRTEEN

BLACKJACK FOREST

The bleak trees of the forest rose three times taller than a man, and they twisted and twined to form an iron-like wall. I reckoned that snakes, possums and hogs might be able to crawl through the scary trees, avoiding their curtain of sharp branches hanging to the ground, but a man wouldn't go very far without being cut to death. Even seeing more than a foot through the dense thicket was hard.

I rode Whistler along the periphery, looking for a way in.

"Willard!" I called from time to time, hoping he might respond.

But I didn't really expect an answer, and I didn't get one. Behind me on the prairie, rolling flashes of lightening crossed the horizon. It was storming somewhere not so far away. Very unnerving. Swallow-tails soared in the sky above, going for the safety of home but lending, with their graceful beauty, a welcome contrast to the bleakness of the looming tangle. Daytime was coming to an end.

Because I was looking up at the sky I was completely surprised by a dreadful figure who popped out of the brush directly into my path. Whistler reared up, and I had to get a handful of his mane to keep from flying off.

"Whoa!" I yelled while flailing around at my belt trying to grab the butt of my pistol.

The ghostly apparition took human form. But instead of attacking me he hunkered down in the gloom and placidly watched my exertions to control my horse. His dirty ragged cloak covered him like a black mackinaw. With a brown slouch hat pulled almost down to his beard he could have been overlooked as a stump had he not made such a dramatic appearance.

Whistler steadied and I found my pistol but didn't unholster it. "Who are you, pardner?" I demanded, my goosebumps subsiding.

"Zechariah," the man declared through his penitent's shroud. It came out deep and significant like it should mean something important. He didn't budge from the ground.

"Is that a name?" I asked.

"That is my name," the gnome said ponderously from under his hat. I'd seen a picture of a gnome in a book of fairy tales which is why I'd thought of it. "And behold, a man riding on a red horse," he proclaimed.

"Is this where you live?" I asked, looking past him at the black forest.

"It is my calling to be here," the gnome replied.

That naturally made me curious. "Who called you to do such as that?" I asked.

"Jesus Christ called me! Who do you think, fool?"

"I'm not such a fool as you," I told him. "I don't live out here in the thorny bushes."

"You may be damned or you may be saved," Zechariah said. "It's up to you. Why don't you get off that horse and we can talk about your soul?"

I declined, remembering what the Indians had said about a strange white holy man who ate human flesh.

"There's a criminal I'm after named Charley Willard," I told him. "His clothes are just about torn off him. Have you seen him?"

"My name means 'God Remembered'," Zechariah explained, picking up the thread of our earlier exchange.

I was intrigued again. "What language is that?" I asked.

Zechariah had to think about it for a minute. "Persian," he said finally.

"That's fine," as if I knew it all along. "Now about this man Willard."

"What's your name?" Zechariah wanted to know.

I told him.

The gnome stood up and dusted his backside. He turned out to be fairly tall but not filled out. I put my hand near my holster again. The scary apparition approached my horse. The visible part of his face was scratched and bleeding, by briars or by fingernails. His smell was strong and even Whistler snorted it off. "That name is not recorded," he whispered. "You weren't sent to patrol this earth."

And you ought to be in the nuthouse, I thought. "I can't waste any more time on this," I told him. He suddenly grabbed Whistler's bridle.

Out came my pistol, and I used it to beat at the fingers which had latched onto the bridle and my leg. This God Remembered had sharp claws and the grip of an eagle. I cocked my Colt and poked it between the prophet's eyes.

Zechariah let loose of both leg and bridle and took a step back, his face contorted in anger.

"You get out of here," he hissed. "Blackjack's gonna get you before you know it. Have you got any bread you can spare?"

My jaw dropped. "What the hell are you doing?" I yelled from the saddle. "Are you wanting to eat me or beg for food?"

"I take what the Lord offers," Zechariah said and he went back to squatting down at the edge of the trees.

"Well, hell, I'll leave you to it." I tapped Whistler with my bootheels and moved around him.

"How 'bout a biscuit?" Zechariah called after me. "Body o' Christ!"

I was shivering but not from the cold. It was getting dark. A faint white slip of a moon was visible in the still-blue sky coming up over the Blackjack. Quite by accident I came upon a tree whose branches had been clumsily snapped. Something had barged into the woods here!

I still had my gun in my hand, and I checked the chambers. They were all loaded, of course. I was scared to go in there, I'll tell you that, but I had no choice if I wanted to live with myself. So I clenched my jaw, draped Whistler's reins over the nearest bush, crouched down and waded slowly into the brush, pushing the thorned branches aside.

After about a dozen cautious steps, with barbs tearing at my cheeks, I came upon a scrap of cloth hanging from a broken twig. A few more steps and I saw what looked like a stain of blood in the dark wet mat of the Blackjack forest's floor. It wouldn't be much further until this search would end one way or the other.

 I didn't give any thought to quitting. My gun hand was sweating, and I kept swapping my revolver back and forth so I could wipe my palms on my pants one at a time. With me on his trail making a tunnel through the thorns, with a crazy Baptist medicine man lurking not far away, and with Indians on the prairie, Willard must know he was a dead man. That didn't mean he would go easy.

The night air didn't stir at all in that lifeless place. I was bleeding from scratches and sweating like a pig. And then I heard a groan.

I squinted through the knife-like branches that were reaching for me and there he was, the body, stretched out on its side, a hat covering the motionless head. The body's shoes were gone and the feet were as bloody as butchered meat. The pants and what was left of his shirt were stained and in tatters. Where the body wasn't leaking dried little red rivers, the skin was burned black as the trees. I took all of this in with one glance.

I stooped over this form, once a live man, cautiously and nudged at the its hat with the barrel of my pistol. The face was revealed, and I knew I had finally found the miserable son of a bitch who had shot Captain Duff off his horse.

CHAPTER FOURTEEN

DELIVERING JUSTICE

Willard was caught. He had already paid a high price for his crimes. His body was worn raw by his run across the unforgiving Florida scrub. But to my reckoning he had not paid nearly enough.

I pressed my cocked revolver into the matted hair sticking out above this sunburned ear and I gave the limp body a sharp kick. Willard groaned again, but he didn't move. "Git up!" I ordered, but it seemed to me that unless the miserable man was the world's greatest actor, all the fight was out of him. I took him to be as near death as he could be and still breathe. But I was taking no chances. Keeping the gun next to Willard's skull, I probed my captive's torn pockets and came up empty.

Disturbing sensations came over me. I might have spat at him. I can't quite recall. "To hell with you," I do remember saying, as if he could hear me. "I guess I'll kill you right now." I aimed my gun straight at him.

But I didn't pull the trigger. Just saying it out loud didn't sound right. It also came to me that I could just allow nature to take its course and let Willard die here all by himself. That would certainly happen, and soon. My conscience said, or the spooks of the Blackjack said, I just needed to get away from my nauseating closeness to Charley Willard to think about this situation.

I forced my way back through the tree branches the way I had come. When I crashed out of the thicket into the open night air I spread my arms to the sky and gulped it in, letting the icy shivers run off my body.

Whistler was where I'd left him, nosing in the undergrowth for shoots of grass like there was neither danger nor death close at hand. Not for the first time, my faithful horse steadied me.

"Reckon we'll camp right here and deal with what's left of that son of a bitch in the morning. Ants and pigs will take care of him for sure." I realized I was speaking aloud to an animal, which was what crazy people did. "Seems like maybe I'm…" I lay my cheek against the smooth chestnut hairs on Whistler's neck and thought about what Captain Duff would do. I took a few deep breaths of horse-scented air and got my mind back in order.

I couldn't just let the man die!

Angrily, I took the coil of rope off the saddle horn, and clutching it in one hand, crawled back into the Blackjack. Willard, of course, was were I'd left him, still bloody and crusty with bugs. The man was breathing, but I didn't care if he was or not. To me he was a dirty piece of rotten meat, but I was going to take him in.

There was no resistance when I tied the rope around his ankles. Back through the trees I went, on hands and knees, pulling the rope along behind me . It reached as far as my stoic horse with more than a yard to spare. I tied it to Whistler's saddle horn, hoisted myself aboard and spurred my mount forward, away from the tangled forest.

The tugging was neither pretty nor smooth, but in time Whistler managed to drag Willard through the brambles. His nasty body came out under the moonlight like on old razorback pulled from the woods. Being hauled across the thorny ground hadn't done him any additional damage that I could see. He was still alive was the main thing.

I untied the rope from the saddle but left Willard's legs bound together. I tied his hands up for extra measure. Now he was stretched out on the ground like a buck deer about to be gutted, his torn fingers pointing back into the Blackjack.

Night having come it was important to make a camp. There was plenty of fuel around for a fire, and before long I had Whistler unsaddled but barely watered, having to suffice from a skin I'd filled up from the Indians' creek. I got a big blaze burning to keep the mosquitos and goblins at bay. Anything that might be left of the boy in me floated away with the smoke into the vast black sky, lit by all the stars and galaxies you might picture. In this night of Florida wildness, I felt all grown up now.

Needing dinner I filled my tin pot with water to boil the grits the girl at the cabin, Clarinda, had given me. There wasn't much left in my canteens, and the last creek was a hike back to where I'd left those Indians, so each drop was precious. Being in a charitable mood I poured much of what remained in one of my two canteens over Willard's face.

He gagged and opened his mouth for more. I obliged and let some water trickle over his lips and down his throat. Willard rolled over and spat. He struggled to raise his head and I gave him a little more. His eyes came open and he stared at mine. I read nothing in his but pain. He swallowed greedily until each drop was gone. Then his head fell back to the earth and his eyes closed.

"That's about all the good works I'm inclined to perform today," I told him.

He surprised me by answering, "He said he was saving me for dinner."

"Good God! Do you mean the preacher?" I exclaimed. Just hearing that sent the same shivers right up my back. But Willard had no more to say.

I concentrated as best I could on boiling my cornmeal, to which I added my last dried chunk of fat bacon. When I considered it tender enough I drank the mush out of the pot and settled back with a handful of the greasy boiled fatback in my sticky fingers, too tired to bother about utensils, too tired to want to think.

In a while the campfire smoke woke me, and I roused up to make a pallet on the ground. There were thunderheads and flashes of lightening to the north but only stars filled our vast sky. My horse snorted contentedly. Willard, all tied up, breathed loudly. A great horned owl began hooting far off in the trees. The cicadas started their song. The buzz of mosquitoes and the hissing of the fire were the only other sounds. But I couldn't sleep.

I had never before understood the full meaning of solitude. Even spending nights in the barn, or wandering in the woods, I had always known that family or friends were nearby. Which somehow got me thinking about Clarinda. In our brief conversation maybe I had bothered her by saying how many girls I had known. All right, I had exaggerated. There really had been only one, Loralie, a bright-eyed teenager whose family lived near the sheriff's house in town. She never paid me a whole lot of attention. Though I was treated by the sheriff's family like one of theirs – well, at least like a distant cousin – it was known that I had been sent away to the farm, so maybe I was disqualified as a beau. While I had tossed and turned on sleepless nights thinking about this girl, her red hair and her shapeliness, on the rare occasions when our paths crossed she pretended I didn't exist. Until one day she changed.

On a rainy Sunday morning, when her family was at their Prince of Peace Episcopal Church in town, Loralie snuck away on her pony and turned up unannounced to visit me in the groves.

Reuben pointed her the way to my barn, and Loralie found me there, soaping up Whistler's leather saddle. Without explanation or hesitation, she sprang off her pony and rushed over to kiss me full on the mouth. I was quite startled but found my hands around her back, fumbling with the buttons on her dress, while she pulled up my shirt. Guided by nature I abandoned the buttons for a more direct approach and raked her hemline up over her fanny while she ground herself into me.

It was so sudden and intense that I experienced the full flood of emotions with my jeans still on. She took notice, of course, gave me a smile with a finger in her mouth and straightened out her dress. With a saucy twitch of her hips she danced out of the barn and was gone.

Brief though it was, that single encounter furnished plentiful fuel for my fantasies for a long time, though, much to my regret, the episode was not repeated.

Clarinda probably wasn't that bold, but there was a directness about her that was both attractive and intimidating. She wasn't at all bad looking. In fact, I imagined that beneath Miss Barlow's worn flannel shirt and dungarees she might have entirely excellent features. Since I was now a serious lawman, I considered her other virtues. The young lady seemed to be a hard worker, and she was a darn good cook. She had a stern look, but maybe that was just when she was talking about Charley Willard and his evil deeds. She might have a pretty smile. Maybe she'd even give me one once she knew I had apprehended Willard. That brought my thoughts back to him, the unconscious body occupying the cold ground near me.

I took a moment to study my captive, laid out on the other side of my campfire. Not much of a man by any count. I guessed that the Indians had forced him into the Blackjack with the expectation that he'd just rot here, or else Zechariah would cannibalize him. Must be something about the cracker they didn't like. I chuckled at that and swallowed the last of my chewy bacon. Maybe I'd never given Indians enough credit for good sense before.

Well, now that I'd rescued Willard from the Blackjack, I guess it was my job to keep him alive. Of course, one reason to keep him kicking was so that I could get answers to a number of questions. Why had this smelly bastard killed Postmaster Abbe? Since nobody had ever claimed that Willard was very smart, there had to be someone else involved. Who put him up to it? And what had he done to Clarinda that made her hate him so much?

"Hello, Gawain MacFarlane." An eerie voice came out of the dark. Zechariah's raspy call got me up to my feet in a hurry.

"I don't want to disturb you," the voice from the woods continued. "Out here in the Blackjack any white man's company is company enough for me. And you can have your prisoner. He's all yours. No hard feelings."

"Get away from here!" I cried into the darkness. By God, I was in a panic! I spun around wildly seeking the source of the voice. "Get away or I'll shoot!" My shout cut through the night, but the sound quickly vanished in the wide starlit prairie.

"You're a good fellow, Gawain," Zechariah said from a slightly different spot in the blackness. "I want you to read your Bible though, every night. This is God Remembered talking."

"I'll read it when it suits me," I sputtered, collecting myself. I had located my pistol and was ready to fire it.

"Have you been saved, son?"

"I don't reckon I have. You get away from me."

There was a moment of silence, then Zechariah spoke from someplace else. "You ought to know the Lord. There's only three ways we get any knowledge. You want to know what they are?"

My heart was beating hard. I took a step into the darkness with my gun pointed at where I thought he was.

"Number one is your senses." The voice came from a new place. "The senses are what you can see and feel. You can probably even smell me."

He did put off an aroma, but it was so strong it seemed to be coming from everywhere.

"Number two is your imagination," Zechariah continued from another spot. I was spinning around. "There's lots you can dream. But your mind can't dream the end of time. You can't wrap your brain around a nothingness beyond the universe, can you? And you can't imagine the infinite." The voice got fainter. "And that's where faith comes in, boy. It's number three. If anything that can exist does exist, you must have faith in an ordering principle. Else you'd go crazy."

"You are crazy!" I swore, pointing my pistol uselessly at phantom shapes in the trees. "I'm going to shoot your mouth shut!" I declared.

"Ride your red steed toward the east," the voice said, and twigs snapped as Zechariah went away.

I was shaking and had trouble breathing. Gradually the songs of a million cicadas restored some sense of peace. But if I'd had trouble sleeping before, I was sure enough wide awake now. I tossed some sticks onto the fire. I checked Willard's bindings, and they seemed secure. The murderer was passed out.

Searching the stars, I wondered if Zechariah was right about infinity and faith. But consider this, Zechariah, if you've got so much faith, how come you're nutty as a loon?

From the saddlebag that was to be my pillow, I chose a book. But not Captain Duff's Bible. I pulled out my father's book of poems. Thumbing through, I got to a new page which I had to strain to see. The beginning was, "*Scots, wha hae wi' WALLACE bled.*" Blood was certainly on my mind. I may have spoken the words softly by the firelight.

Scots, wham Bruce has often led
Welcome to your gory bed,
    Or to Victorie!
Now's the day and now's the hour;
See the front of battle lour;
See approach proud EDWARD's power –
    Chains and Slaverie!

Wha will be a traitor knave?
Wha can fill a coward's grave?
Wha sae base as be a slave?
    Let him turn and flee!
Wha for Scotland's King and Law,
Freedom's sword will strongly draw,
FREE-Man stand or FREE-Man fa'
    Let him follow me!

Under the moonlight, by a dying fire, I was entranced by imagined pictures of leather and homespun clad men trotting in an irregular formation across grassy fields making their heroic charge, bugles blaring, at the armies of the tyrannical king. Which king I knew not, but . . . . Resting my revolver, my "Freedom's sword," on my chest, I fell into fitful sleep.

I had bad dreams and woke up in a cold sweat, thankful to see the moon descending. The dawn would come soon. I rubbed the sleep from my eyes. Looking over the dead fire, I caught Willard, still flat on the ground, watching me.

CHAPTER FIFTEEN

BACK TO THE WORLD
WITH MY PRISONER

The sun was coming up and it took all of my strength to lift my prisoner and deposit him belly-down on Whistler, across the saddle. Never before nor since have I been so grateful to leave a place as I was to say goodbye to the Blackjack.

Step-by-step I led my faithful horse through the sharp grass across the prairie and finally back to the muddy shore of the Peace River. I paused at the bank only long enough to top my canteens and allow Whistler to drink his belly full before, following the slow-moving stream eastward, we again found ourselves at the ferry landing.

There was quite a bustle at the crossing. Last night's rain, which had missed the Blackjack, had swollen the river, and there was a queue of wagons carrying crates of sweet potatoes, pulled by teams of mules, waiting to get across. The drovers were in the process of reorganizing themselves after having ridden across the water on horseback alongside their wagons which had been brought over one-at-a-time on the ferry.

The strange man who ran the operation was in conversation with the head of the party when I emerged from the woods leading Whistler.

The teamsters and the ferry proprietor took an immediate interest in the load I had slung over the saddle. They came over to inspect the body.

"Would that be your Charley Willard?" the ferryman asked.

I nodded. "He's gonna need a doctor probably, to get him ready to hang."

"The nearest doctor's in Fort Ogden," the ferry owner told me. The wagon boss nodded thoughtfully. He appeared to be a farmer, sweat coming through his shirt and staining the brim of his brown felt hat.

"I know about this person," the farmer said. His words came out slow as a sermon. "They say he killed the Yankee postmaster up in Sarasota."

"He did that," I confirmed, "and I plan to take him up to the courthouse in Pine Level for trial."

"You do?" the man said, making it a question. Her paused and crossed his arms. "Well down here in Fort Ogden there's quite a few who says he did the right thing." Finished, he stuck out his chin.

"I don't plan to go through Fort Ogden," I replied, though in fact that had been my expected route. It was on the most direct road north.

"Which way will you go?" he asked, watching my face and making me uncomfortable.

"What do you care?" I asked him back.

"Who the hell are you?" he demanded, suddenly affronted.

I tugged at my collar to show him my badge. "I'm a Deputy Sheriff, and I'll have you stand out of my way if you can't be of any help to me."

I turned my back on him and went about pulling Willard off my saddle and laying him out on the sand. "I'll need a bucket of water for this man and some corn for my horse. And I need to borrow one of them wagons." I pointed to the corral.

The ferryman thought a moment and decided to cooperate. "Ain't nothin' for free around here," he muttered as he fetched the water. The farmer and his cowboys broke up and got their own rigs underway, headed upriver toward Fort Ogden. "There goes trouble," the ferryman said. "They're some cheap sonabitches. I ain't that trusting of your deputy credentials," he added.

"I'm deputized and I need that wagon, and that's all there is to it," I told him. "There's a reward for this here Willard, and when I collect it I'll come back and give you fifteen dollars for the rig."

"And what if you don't come back."

"Then you can find me," I said. "I won't be far away. I'm starting to feel right at home in this country."

"There could be something wrong with your brains, son. How much reward are they offering for that man?"

"I don't know that for certain, but it ought to be a good one for killing a U.S. Postmaster and shooting the top Deputy Sheriff of this county."

I made my deal with the proprietor and got Whistler hooked up to the best of the shabby wagons. I dumped the insensible Willard in the back, and the ferryman hauled us across the river on his barge. I had in mind a better destination than Fort Ogden.

The sun was perched just above the pine trees when I steered my wagon into the Barlow yard where a great drama was in progress. The old man was trying to contain a bonfire he'd been feeding with cabbage palm logs as long as he was tall. The project was aimed at clearing his field, but towering flames were whipping up into the tree tops.

Clarinda, was at the well, pumping up kegs of water. Her hands flew to her hair when she saw me, a good sign.

"Hello, Clarinda," I hailed her. "It's me again."

"I can see who you are!" she shouted. "Better not unhitch that wagon. You're just in time to see this whole place go up in smoke."

Nevertheless, I coaxed Whistler ahead and tied him to a porch rail. "Your pa's got a pretty big blaze going there," I observed. "The breeze is picking up. Likely he should let her die down."

"He just gets crazy sometimes," she said angrily, wiping her hands on her dress. "Where'd you get the wagon?"

"Over at the Peace River. Man let me have it for a piece of the reward."

"What reward is that?" she asked hopefully.

"Come see."

Full of curiosity, Clarinda hurried over to look into the wagon, and then recoiled as if she'd stuck her hand in a hornet's nest.

"He's not daid?" she asked.

"Close to it but not quite, I'd say. Let's splash some water on him and see if he comes to."

"I don't want him to come to! Get him away from here!" Her face was pinched in anger and fear.

"He ain't going to hurt nobody. At least not today." I climbed down from the wagon and fetched a water keg to pour it over my prisoner's face.

Willard choked and groaned. He turned over, breathing hard.

"Man's about had it," I said.

"You ought to take him over to Horse Creek and dump him in. Be done with him."

"I don't like him either, but what was it he ever did to you?"

"I can't tell you that. It's too shameful. But get him away from here!"

"I plan to take him with me to Pine Level. I can be on my way now, or I can help you put out that fire."

That got her attention. "Pa, it's getting away!" she screamed.

Indeed, fingers of fire were snaking across the rough sedge toward the house, and flurries of sparks were whirling about it the air.

We grabbed for hoes and shovels and ran to help the old man fight the flames. Pa Barlow was pretty well worn out by that time, covered in sweat and ashes. But the three of us furiously raked and slapped at the burn as it spread in the grass. After a futile hour it was pure luck that the wind decided to die down and give us a break. The fire was by no means extinguished, but it had decided on its own to rest in its current location.

I heard Whistler's whinny, and over my shoulder saw Willard trying to crawl up onto the front of the wagon and grasp for the reins.

I cursed more than I'm used to, trying to run and at the same time get my large Colt from its holster which in my exertions had worked itself around to the back of my trousers.

Whistler with the wagon was loping for the trees, away from the still glowing field.

I stuck two fingers into my mouth and produced a monumental piercing screech, the intent of which was known to Whistler. My good horse came to a halt and looked back to see what I wanted. Still tangled in his ropes, Willard spilled out of the wagon.

I had my gun out when I caught up to him. Recognizing his predicament, Willard decided to play possum. He crossed his eyes and went limp, and I had to pile him like a sack of potatoes back into the wagon's bed.

He was, however, alert enough to mumble, "Give me something to eat, I beg you."

"I'll give you what you gave Captain Duff. A belly full of bushwhacker shot."

Willard seemed to pass out again. He went to mumbling about "damn snakes." I got him and the buggy back to the porch rail where I unhitched Whistler and led him well away from the wagon so that Willard would have to cross some ground to steal him.

The fire in the field still needed watching, and it was dark. We were all well tired before it was safely contained.

"This sure puts me behind schedule," I said to Clarinda, shaking the ashes out of my hair. "I hate to be on the road with that skunk after nightfall. He's got friends in this part of the county."

"Then you'll just have to spend the night here," she piped up, just as I had hoped. "Would that be alright with you, Pa?" she called.

The old man nodded his head gratefully. He was covered in soot, as were we all. "I'll just sit out here for a few and watch over these coals," he wheezed.

"Thank you for the hospitality," I said. "I best get something for my man to eat. Do you have anything you could spare?"

Clarinda scowled. She went into the cabin alone where she found a pot of corn grits, cold and solid, on the sideboard of her stove. She carried it outside and handed it to me.

"That's all we got at the moment," she said. It was a dreary meal, but I took it to the pump, swished some well water into the pot and stirred it for my prisoner's consumption. I got Willard upright, hands still tied behind him, and slapped a big spoonful of the cold porridge into his open mouth. He worked it around and swallowed it down, so I slapped in some more until it was gone. "That'll have to do you till morning," I said, and pushed him back over onto his side. "We ain't got fancy accommodations here."

Not taking any more chances, I borrowed a length of chain from old man Barlow's shed and used it to attach Willard to the wagon itself. Barlow generously brought a bucket of corn to the coral. Whistler got a better supper than my prisoner had.

Clarinda went into the cabin shaking debris off her clothes. We started to follow her in, but she ordered both of to wait in the yard while she cleaned herself up. Her dad started to protest but her look made him think better of it, and he instead sank wearily into a chair on the porch.

"That was sure something," he said, wiping his eyes.

"Came close to getting away from you," I agreed.

"That would have just been my luck. But I'm trying my hardest to get that field ready so I can put in a crop next month and get us a decent supply of potatoes and beans and greens. It won't take me long to make a garden and enough extra to sell if I can just get this place plowed."

"What are you living on now, if you don't mind me asking."

"The honest truth is we've about eat all our sweet potatoes and so it's come down to cabbage palm stew and me trapping squirrels. Clarinda raised some pigs. We killed two and smoked 'em, and we still got some of that. I sold the rest. Then somebody stole our old sow."

"Stole it?"

"She didn't walk out that gate by herself, did she?" He was indignant.

"You know who stole her?" I inquired.

"We're kind of beyond civilization here, son. There ain't no law but what you make it."

Well, I thought, I'm a deputy, but I didn't make my point because I had no time to be chasing after hog thieves.

Clarinda finally let us come inside. She had washed herself with a tin pan of water, tied her hair up in a blue bandana, and put on a clean dress. And she had fried up some supper.

"Pork chops, biscuits and grits. Help yourself while it's here," she announced.

Her pa grinned. "We sure do eat a whole lot better when you come around, young man," he told me.

We ate greedily and washed it down with some kind of tea Clarinda said came from orange peels.

"I guess I better go check on my prisoner." I patted my stomach contentedly and pushed back the table. "That was a fine meal, Clarinda."

Just hearing me say her name made her blush. "I'll clear away these dishes and come join you," she said, "but I won't go near that man."

"I'm gonna find me something to smoke if it's just dried palmetto berries," Mr. Barlow muttered. He went to poking around in the corners of the house.

After I put up Whistler, I administered another cup of water to Willard, who was breathing steadily and looking ever so much better than he was letting on.

"Riding in this old wagon must suit you," I said, making a jest. "I ought to let you walk tomorrow." Willard answered me by snoring loudly.

The cabin door opened and closed quietly and Clarinda came outside. She came near enough to get a peek at his sleeping form, but the sight of him caused her to shudder and turn away. "He's just like the slimy snakes he hates," she said under her breath.

"What's that?" I asked.

"Snakes worry him. That's the kind of gutless coward he is. Let's go somewhere else."

The two of us walked out to the field to inspect what remained of the fire. The moon was coming up, and the shadows it cast, as well as those from the flickering embers, made the ground seem to dance around us.

"That fool Charley Willard once told me he'd killed seven men, not counting niggers," she said breaking the silence.

"Not counting!" I exclaimed. "You taught me something about that scoundrel's nature, right there!"

"That's not a human's nature," she said.

"Well, I don't believe anybody would make that up, would they?"

"That's not what I meant," she said. "It ain't the way a human acts. It's the way the Devil acts."

"I don't know much about the Devil, but I'm learning some more about a really bad man!"

"I told you to just put a bag over his head and drop him in the creek. Or you could forget about the bag."

I had thought of doing something similar, but replied, "Then I'd be just as bad as him."

"No, you could never be as bad as him." She sounded like she had known me for a long time.

"What's your grievance against Charley?" I asked her again.

Instead of answering, she changed the subject. "Gawain, tell me about your father and your mother."

"I never knew my mother," I explained. "She died giving birth to me. I have a photograph of her. She was pretty. And I only have a few memories of my father. He died when I was four years old 'cause of wounds he got in the War. In my memories, he was in bed most of the time. A nursemaid looked after him and me. She was a Confederate widow, I think. They say my dad was in a lot of pain and took morphine, or something like it."

"Well, at least your ma and pa had you and gave you the gift of life."

That softened me up. "That's a pretty thing to say," I told her. "They did that, despite my dad having a lot of shrapnel in him from where he was shot off a horse charging a gun battery in Tennessee. And the horse got killed and fell over on him. That's what I was told by the sheriff and by Captain Duff, both of whom was there."

"That's terrible." Clarinda had tried to imagine what a war was like but she really couldn't.

"Sheriff Sandy Watson raised me," I added.

"And Mrs. Watson. Did she raise you, too?"

"Yes and no. She never did seem to warm up to me. She never said she disliked me, or anything like that. But she didn't seem happy to have me around. So I mostly stayed out at the farm we had where we raised about a hundred acres of oranges and lemons. Mrs. Watson passed away herself last year, and I guess I'll keep living on the farm."

"My mother ran off. She left me a pretty dress but she didn't say goodbye. Now it's just me and Pa."

"I thought you said she was dead."

Clarinda turned her head away.

"Why did she run off?" I asked her.

"I don't know. We're poor folks, and I suppose she didn't want to stay poor. They was always fighting. When I was little I'd have to go outside and hide. They'd fight over anything."

"Someday they'll fight wars over who owns the moon," I said – I don't know why since this idea had never occurred to me before. Yet it drew her attention up to the sky and the grandeur of nature, to great gray clouds floating across the stars in the moonlight. And just on impulse Clarinda stood on her tiptoes and kissed me.

I think that surprised us both. She started to break away and run back to the house, but I restrained her long enough to kiss her back.

"Fresh!" she cried. Then she was gone.

I slept that night in their barn, with their cow, dreaming about you can guess what.

I woke up before the first sunlight and found her standing over me. "You snore," she said.

CHAPTER SIXTEEN

CLARINDA RIDES ALONG

When I set out at daybreak with Willard, Clarinda came along. I didn't invite her, and she didn't ask. She just slid out of the cabin carrying a bag of clothes, saddled up her own horse and slung a lever-action shotgun across her lap. I was all for it, I guess, but too dumb to know what to say, so I kept my mouth shut.

The old man watched silently from the doorway. I think he had been expecting something like this. In my considered opinion, he knew she was stuck on me like nobody's business.

"I'll be back before long and bring you some seedlings to plant in that field you're clearing," she yelled from atop her horse. He nodded and watched us go. Her horse was named Daisy.

Willard had revived some and sat cross-legged in the back of the wagon, still tied hand and foot. His face was burnt red and covered in cuts above his whiskers. But the cuts were healing-over. He stared dully out the back of the wagon at the receding homestead and the same familiar featureless country. We were all tired of it. The scenery was limited to more grassland and more palmetto scrub and the occasional stray cow grazing alone on the prairie, watching us pass.

After a mile, I stopped the wagon.

"We'll let your horse do the pullin' for a while," I told Clarinda "and I'll ride on Whistler, unless you object to that." These were the first words either of us had spoken.

I thought she might object, unhappy about losing her mount, but she decided to let me be in charge on this trip, or to think I was. Nicely, she said, "Let me help you unhitch ol' Whistler."

We switched out the horses, and Clarinda took over the wagon. "I've seen 'em built with springs under the seat," she said, her complaint softened by a smile.

"Well, this one weren't, and you feel every rock in the road," I told her.

On Whistler I alternated between following behind the wagon, so as to keep an eye on Willard, and trotting ahead so that I could scout out any problems. It was lonely country, a vast unpopulated space full of flocks of birds and wildlife, like raccoons, gopher tortoises, deer and bear that you wouldn't necessarily see in the daylight, but you could spot their prints and their scat. Over everything was a brilliant blue sky with huge cottony clouds low on the tree line and that big white pearl of a sun that made the horizon shimmer. We didn't pass a house or see a person after leaving the Barlow farm.

I returned from a swing up ahead and reported, "There's a crossroads in about a mile and a stream where we can cool off." I stopped to let

Clarinda pass. Falling into step with the slow pace of the rattling wagon I caught Willard's attention.

"Got anything to say for yourself?" I inquired.

He was dulled some by our bumpy ride, but moved his chin an inch to keep me in view. "You can get screwed," he said, quite plainly.

"Glad you're feeling better. What did Abbe ever do to you?" I asked.

"Damn sonofabitch thought he could run over anybody he wanted," Willard spat out.

"What's that supposed to mean?" I pressed him. "How was he trying to run over you?"

But Willard had said his piece and closed his eyes. "I need to piss," he said.

The trail got wider as we approached the headwaters of Horse Creek. Someone had tossed up a rickety bridge over the water. It was constructed out of pine logs with warped boards nailed across them. We clippity-clopped across it, but on the other side I asked Clarinda to pull over so we could give the horses a rest.

She steered the rig off to one side and stretched out the crick in her back, then climbed down from the wagon. There was shade under the oak trees growing beside the water, nourished by the stream's overflow in the rainy season.

A hand pump was bolted to the bridge and its pipe was sunk in the creek, some cattleman's donation to the range. There was an old rusty bucket hanging on it. I dismounted. Willard's head rolled from side to side, sizing up our surroundings in the glade.

I inspected the pump. "Wonder if this thing works." I gave it a few energetic cranks, and a bit of creek water spurted out the tap. "Whew! That saves us from having to unhitch your horse. And it gives time for Mister Willard to go out in the bushes, if he is so inclined."

I filled the bucket and placed it below her horse's nose. "Whistler can drink his fill out of the creek. But you best keep Daisy's bucket full."

"Yes, sir," she muttered to herself. "And I guess I'll find some bushes of my own."

I led Whistler through the trees to the narrow waterside where he noisily buried his mouth in the stream. Then I returned to the wagon for Willard.

To this day I don't know how he did it. Maybe he used some rusty nail he'd worked loose from the floor boards. But he had got himself loose and out of the wagon and had taken hold of Clarinda from behind. She was struggling with him, but he managed to pin her wrists with one hand and get a hold of her shotgun with the other.

I took in our predicament, and his. I didn't think he could work the shotgun's lever or pull the trigger without letting her go, and I told him so. We were at a standoff.

"You put your hand on your pistol, and I'm sure as hell gonna try!" he yelled at me. We were facing each other with the road between us.

"Let's talk about this," I said and held up my hands.

"Nothin' to talk about. Toss your gun on the ground if you value this girl's life."

"That ain't the way it's going to be, Charley. I don't want to shoot you. You know I've had every chance to do that. But I will if I have to and this revolver of mine will put such a big hole in whatever part of you I hit - even if it's just side meat - that you will be dead. So let' talk."

I could see his small brain working.

"Damn you!" he said. "Let's talk about me getting in that wagon and riding out of here."

Clarinda was trying to twist around and bite him, but even sick he was a powerful man and held her tightly.

"Maybe you could," I said. "Maybe you deserve a break. Somebody had to have put you up to killing Mr. Abbe. You're not the kind of man who would do that on his own."

"Hell, yes, they put me up to it! It was never my idea!" Willard was excited, and feverish, no doubt. "It was Bidwell's idea. And Dr. Andrews' idea! It was the whole Sarasota Vigilante Society's idea. They're all way more guilty than me."

I didn't know yet what any of that meant, but I said, "Then turn the girl loose, and let's go and tell your story to the judge. Straight up, Charley. Man to man."

"Hell no!" he hollered." He wasn't buying it. I thought I might be able to shoot him in the shoulder at least, but there was the danger of hitting Clarinda.

"Hell no, is right!" Clarinda hollered back, and she managed to kick her leg behind herself and catch him in the nuts with her boot heel. His mouth fell open and he let her go and stumbled backwards. She spun around and got him again in the same place with the pointy toe of her boot this time. Willard took a knee, and I rushed in to disarm him of that shotgun. Before he could catch his breath I had him trussed up like a Christmas turkey and sprawled face down on the ground.

Clarinda gave him another kick in the gut and would have kept at it but I stopped her. I won't repeat the swear words she directed at Charley Willard, and at me for tying such poor knots in the first place. She had to lean against a tree to get herself calmed down. I hauled Willard back into the wagon.

I gave Clarinda the reins, mounted up on Whistler, and after some recriminations we were on our way again.

She wasn't ready to speak to me yet, so I struck up a conversation with Willard. I even got into the bed of the wagon with him.

I told Charley that in my view, his only chance of not being hung was to come clean about the whole affair. To tell everything he knew about the "Assassination Society," I called it. Like I was killing time, I pulled out my king snake and massaged it. The varmint was quite docile if you knew how to hold it and got content by wrapping itself all around my arm. Willard was transfixed by this, and he started trembling.

I'll never know if Willard told me everything, but he told me a lot. I poured some water on him to help him go on. Clarinda was listening, too, and while I played with the snake in front of his fascinated eyes we got an earful, about the whole plot and the people involved – all of whom, in Willard's view, had deserted and betrayed him.

The snake went back in the bag, and an hour later we pulled into the town of Pine Level, which consisted of a handful of houses and a church, all scattered around the new courthouse which itself was a bare-bones affair. That courthouse was the principal reason for Pine Level's existence. The hamlet lacked a railroad or a navigable river or even a crossroads. The small community's only lifeline was the parade of lawyers and judges who had to travel into the backwoods when court was in session. This happened twice a year, each term being for ten days.

Inside the courthouse I found the office of the clerk, who was sitting at an oak desk in the middle of a stack of record books. Keeping him company was one of Sheriff Watson's deputies, the jailer actually, his boots propped up on a counter. After introducing myself, I announced that I had brung in Postmaster Abbe's murderer, Charley Willard, to be bound over in the jail.

The deputy came to attention and followed me to see the prisoner.

"He's one dirty sonofabitch," the jailer observed. "Where'd you catch him? In an outhouse?"

"I guess I probably don't smell that good myself."

"Your girlfriend in the wagon don't seem the kind who'd care." Clarinda was perched on the wagon seat with a shotgun on her lap. With her hair bundled under her hat and baggy shirt and jeans, she looked the epitome of a wild frontier rustic.

"To hell with that talk," I told him.

The deputy was anxious to hear my account of Willard's capture, and he helped escort the prisoner around back to the jail. Willard was happy to walk now and be away from me and that snake.

This jail would be hard to believe today. It was a two-story structure but only about ten feet square. The upstairs, where the prisoners slept, was accessed by a ladder propped up against the side of the building. The deputy explained that it was removed at night so that prisoners couldn't escape.

"It'll only be Willard in there tonight," he told me. "The other man, Joe Anderson, got bailed out."

"By who?" I demanded. I knew that name. It was Joe Anderson's shotgun that Willard had used to kill the postmaster.

"That lawyer Bartholomew went his bail. Don't know who put up the money, but Bartholomew's the one brought it in. You and the lady can stay right here in the courthouse tonight if you want. Reasonable rates."

"No, sir. I got to reach Manatee City and report to Sheriff Watson, now that I'm shet of this outlaw."

The jailer did at least give me some information about the condition of the roads and where they went. "It's quite a ways to where's you're goin'," he commented.

Clarinda and I conferred about it and decided that we would best travel out of the tiny town together and try to reach a spot known as old Myakka Village, where the road was said to fork, before stopping to camp. When morning came, I would ride one way north to Manatee City to find the sheriff, and she would take the wagon the other way west to Sarasota, where we would reunite as soon as I could get there. It seemed natural to assume that we would be meeting again. But first we had to do some traveling. Our respective destinations were each more than forty miles away.

I bought some bacon and a can of beans at the small store across from the courthouse, right next to the Methodist Church. It was gathering dusk when we left Pine Level and it would be dark when we got to old Myakka Village.

JAILER'S STORY

We don't have too many prisoners down here in our jail. My job is doing nothing most of the time. Sheriff Watson inherited me, you might say. He kept me on when he took over from Sheriff Cicero Hayman, but the job don't pay a whole lot. Truth is, I don't get paid at all unless there's a prisoner to look after. I raise pigs at the house, and I tend a garden, and I could spend all my time out there except the wife kind of runs our house and it makes her a lot happier when I'm not under her feet, she says. So, I sit around the courthouse, in case there's any need for my services. I do wear a badge.

Sometimes people come in to the office mad about something or another, and it smooths everyone's feelings when they see me in charge. Of course, the clerk is in charge, but the law has to be in evidence. When there is a prisoner, usually a hog thief, or a cow thief, or some drunk bootlegger who shot somebody, I get the jail sorted out, cleaned up, get 'em some grub from my ol' lady, and explain the rules. The main one is, Shut Up! I don't like no yelling or bellyaching. And you get a bucket of water and a bucket for your night soil, and you get whatever my wife cooks – the five cents the county pays for a meal ain't much - and if it's burned and tough or too greasy to suit you, or you don't have a blanket or a lovely softy bed, I could give a shit. But if you got the money, honey, we can fix you up. I'm the law down here, when the sheriff ain't around.

If your people have some dough, things will get a lot better – just as good as you want to pay for. If you're staying more than a day or two, I'd recommend arranging help from your folks. A dumb cracker like Charley Willard, he'll get my wife's cooking. Them eggs may be watery and cold, and the meat might have turned a little sour. But it won't kill you. Calling it crap won't help a bit. Unless your kin want to chip in. Whatever they want to provide for you is okay as far as I'm concerned, so long as they remember to provide something for me.

CHAPTER SEVENTEEN

OUR CAMPFIRE

This night would be the first time in four long days that I had not had Charley Willard with me, in spirit or in the putrid flesh. And it would be Clarinda's first night, ever, spent away from her pa and her home, such as it was.

That sense of freedom affected us both, and as I rode on Whistler and she drove the wagon, we were uncommonly quiet. In time, however, we had songbirds for company. Clarinda could pick out the "see you, see yer," of the meadowlark, the "drink your tea" of the towhee, and the "how are you? I'm fine," of the vireo, and she entertained me with her imitations. We reached the creek as the sun's last glow turned the sandy shore a rich golden color. The road dipped into the water, and I rode into it to verify that it was shallow enough and the bottom solid enough for the wagon to get across. There was no sign of a town.

"Why don't we just make camp here?" Clarinda called after me. She was more than tired after a long day in the wagon.

"Suits me," I replied. While her horse, Daisy, drank its fill of the clear creek water, I scouted upstream a few hundred feet to find a likely spot on the bank to make a camp. Out of sight of the road, I found a sandy beach nestled against the willows on the bank and the charred remnants of an old campfire. It appeared suitable so I rode back to lead Daisy and the wagon up the lazy current.

I eventually learned that had we continued a little further on the road, we would have soon discovered that this old Myakka Village was actually a little settlement of vegetable-patch farmers and flower gardeners near the shallow headwaters of the stream by which we were camping. By luck, the spot we picked was far nicer and more private than anything we would have found in the village itself.

We built a campfire first thing, while the horses cooled their hooves in the water. Clarinda laid out our provisions on a saddle blanket, the bacon and beans I had bought, a bag of cornmeal she had brought along, and a pot and pan tied to Whistler's saddle.

I watched Clarinda go down to the water to fill the pot. Her strong, long legs in those worn blue jeans gave me some motivating ideas about how this unusual evening might progress.

"I want to wash up," she said when she got back. "And I suggest you might want to do the same."

"And how would that work?" I asked.

"I'm going to wade around that bend where it's private. What you do is up to you." She gathered up her little pack of clothes and sundries and went down to the water, stripping off her shoes when she got there and waded out of sight.

"Well, damn," I thought. A bath on this long trip had not really crossed my mind, but it had been more than a week. "I guess I do smell pretty rank," I admitted. I hadn't packed a change of clothes but decided that a swim might feel pretty good after all. So I stripped and slid into the water in front of the camp. As the moon came up I thought I caught a glimpse of Clarinda's white-as-linen body around the bend. Being a polite young man, I turned away. By the time I turned back again the vision was gone. I was laying on my back, relaxing into the sandy bottom and the cool leaf scented water, when I saw her return on the beach wearing a white dress. She called out my name.

I stood up naked as I was born, covering myself a little, and she squealed and averted her eyes.

"You can just go ahead and fix our supper, Clarinda. Don't mind me at all."

"You get some clothes on right now if you want to eat."

"I'm getting' hungry, but it ain't for beans," I thought to myself. But I pulled on my pants, which were stiff and shaped like the back of a horse. I wrapped my shirt around my chest.

Clarinda was sitting on the blanket, all clean in her soft dress a little too big for her, and all I could think to say when I knelt beside her was, "You're sure pretty."

She set the pot with the cornmeal on the fire and opened up the can of beans while I sat back and watched. I think she was well aware of the effect she was having on me here in our wilderness. She smiled to herself, which suggested that she was not too unpleased with what she had seen of me. The birds were singing all around us.

"I guess you think you're mighty swell," she said as she stirred the pot. "Catching a criminal and then walking around here naked in the woods."

"I think I'm mighty swell being here with you," I said and lightly traced her ankles with my fingertips.

"What are you up to, Gawain?" She turned toward me and placed a soft hand on my cheek.

"Thoughts I haven't had before," I said truthfully. I reached out and took her in my arms. She hesitated only a moment, then rolled into my embrace. I kissed her neck.

The fire hissed and popped an ember at her dress. Clarinda gasped and jumped up, being sure the fabric hadn't been burned.

"You could just take that off," I suggested softly. Clarinda crossed her arms and looked up at the moon. She stretched slowly. She let her dress fall to the ground. I could not believe my good luck.

The sight of Clarinda's pale body in the moonlight was the most beautiful vision I'd ever seen in my life. She stood silently as my eyes drifted slowly down, across her white breasts, the swell of her hips and the downy place between her legs. She shivered slightly and I rose quickly to fold her into the warmth of my arms.

"Are you sure about this, Clarinda?" I whispered in her ear, saying a silent prayer that she was. In answer, she pressed her body closer into my mine, leaving no doubt what she was feeling. I lowered her carefully to the ground – she had become precious and suddenly fragile-seeming to me. I shed my pants and knelt beside her, taking her hands, rough from manual labor, and pressing them to my face. In my own mind, I wasn't too sure what a young man in my position was supposed to do. I knew what I wanted to do, but I just wasn't sure of the correct way to approach it. Was there a correct way? I sure didn't want to make a mistake now and ruin what we'd started.

Clarinda took care of that, in the way she took care of so many things. She pulled me closer and I could feel her naked body along the length of mine. I kissed her, trying to be gentle at first, but then she wound her arms around my neck and pulled my chest into her breasts. Being gentle became less the object. I slid over on top of her and Clarissa raised her knees. I felt the hot dampness of her thighs against my burning skin. Things got much simpler after that.

That was the first time; the first time for me, the first time for her, the first time for us together. We made love again that night, and in the morning, and in the warmth of the day before we finally broke camp. We must have made love a thousand times since then. Maybe, at least I hope, I've become better at it. I don't need any guidance anymore, that's for sure. But no matter how many times we've laid together, that first time stays etched in my mind: the river bank, Clarinda's white dress, the moon above, and two young people finding love and bliss in each other's arms. For that, above all else, I am thankful.

CHAPTER EIGHTEEN
HOW IT ENDS

Joseph Anderson, the owner of the gun which had allegedly been used to commit murder and damn near kill the Captain, had refused to say anything of significance while being transported to the jail in Pine Level after his arrest by the sheriff. As I've heard it, all he would say was, "I've got important friends who won't like me being disgraced like this. I need to speak to my lawyer." He refused to tell who his lawyer was, which was an obstacle to fulfilling his request.

Captain Duff, still recuperating, learned about Anderson's stubbornness from the sheriff. He determined to ride down to Pine Level and interrogate the man. Since Duff didn't know what had become of me, he hoped he might get some clues from Anderson about Willard's escape route and possibly my whereabouts somewhere in the wilderness.

Sheriff Watson had no objection, except that Duff still had bandages wrapped around his shoulder and chest, walked haltingly, and was bled out pale as a ghost. The Captain's wife, Ellen, had those objections and more, which she expressed loudly. "Well darlin," he told her, "I'm feeling a lot better than I look, and I'm a tough old bird."

"You can barely put your pants on," she declared. "I'm watching you. How are you going to saddle your horse? How are you…?" He put a finger to her lips. "I'll be just fine. Trust me on this one," he said softly.

Had Captain Duff waited another day to begin his ride to Pine Level, he might have learned, though the roundabout telegraph line that went from Pine Level to Arcadia, and from there to Lakeland, then to Tampa, and finally to an unattended desk at what would become the railroad station in Braidentown/Manatee City, that Joe Anderson had been bailed out of the jail. But he would also have learned that Charley Willard had been brought in. As it was, Duff didn't get that news until he rode into the quiet village of Pine Level the next day and found out that he had just missed me, and that I was traveling with some girl the jailer couldn't name.

Duff took a moment to recover from his ride and examine his bandages in the privacy of the jail's outhouse. Grimacing, he yanked off the soiled linen and threw it into the hole. At his wife's insistence, he had brought with him a few yards of fresh dressing, and he wrapped most of that around his chest. He changed his shirt and took a drink from the bottle of pain medicine his doctor had prescribed. Somewhat restored, he decided to interrogate the jail's only prisoner, Charley Willard.

Rather than being held upstairs, which would have required the jailer to deal with the ladder, Charley Willard was housed downstairs. It was a bare, functional room, but it wasn't so bad. There was a wooden floor and a barred window through which air could circulate. Willard had a cot. He had promised the jailer that his fiancé was coming to deliver some financial support. Therefore a doctor had attended to him, courtesy of the county. Willard was sitting on the bed rocking back and forth, lost in whatever thoughts he had, when the jailer let Captain Duff enter the cell. The prisoner noted his arrival and turned around to face his visitor. Both men fixed their eyes on the other, and Willard was the first one who spoke.

"Didn't mean to shoot you," he told the deputy.

"That's bullshit," Duff told him. "But I reckon that's what you are, a born bullshitter."

"Not true," Willard said, and spread out his hands as an apology. "The gun just went off."

"No one will ever believe that, least of all me. But here you sit, and I expect you'll hang for shooting the postmaster, not for nearly killing me. It would make a lot more sense to everybody if you told the reason why you did it."

"I'm innocent of the crime," the prisoner said, his eyes wide open and his expression earnest. "As God is my witness."

"Have mercy, Son!" Duff exclaimed. "The Lord shouldn't have to hear such blasphemy as that. Hanged is one thing, but you'll be bound for Hell for uttering profanity against the Lord!"

Willard stared down at his tortured feet, the bandages black from walking about in his cell. "I'm just telling the truth," he insisted, though his voice wasn't convincing.

"If that's your line, you'll have to explain it to your Maker, not to me." Duff got up and pushed open the jail's heavy wooden door. "I'm done," he told the jailer, who had been standing outside the door trying to overhear their conversation.

"That boy don't talk much," the jailer complained.

"No, he don't," Duff agreed, getting up on his horse and trying not to show any pain. "Maybe he'll open up when they finally put a rope around his ornery scrawny neck."

Clarinda and I lingered by the creek in the morning. Most of the day, in fact. It was late afternoon when we finally departed camp. In less than a mile we reached the little town where the road forked.

"It's about twenty more miles to Sarasota," I told her, "but the road is supposed to be good. You'll probably see people on the way if you should need any help. Keep a steady pace and you ought to be to town not long after dark."

"I'll be fine," she told me. "And if night falls I'm used to being under God's stars. Just you come back to me." She opened her arms, and I bent down from my horse to give her a kiss. "Hurry up," I said, "and I'll see you tomorrow as soon as I can get there." We were suddenly like lovers in a book of poetry.

I watched her clatter off westward down the road, wondering what kind of woman, what kind of girl, I had gotten mixed up with. Should I have let her go off alone? She didn't seem afraid. She'd been raised in the woods, and she knew how to use that lever-action. Whistler was certain all would be well, and I spurred him up the north fork toward Bradentown.

Clarinda took it easy, letting Daisy pick her own pace as the stray sounds from old Myakka Village disappeared and the road became hers alone.

She liked the nighttime best. That's probably part of the reason she had let Gawain draw her to him. With the moon, the fireflies, and sweet air. This morning, this whole day, had been so nice. Now the road smelled of baked grass and soggy bottom land. She was nearing civilization. And she was actually a bit sleepy. To rest her eyes, she closed them for just a second, long enough for the swaying wagon to lull her to sleep.

She was abruptly awakened by the shouts of cowboys who were circling a wildly blazing cabin set far back in the fields. Flames rose and popped and crackled, and riders darted around the fire, yelling and firing off guns.

Clarinda quickly collected herself and, believing this was no business of hers, snapped the reins at Daisy to hurry past this catastrophe, or battle, or drunkenness, or whatever it might be. She thought she had gotten safely by it all when suddenly she heard the thundering hooves of their horses and the riders were upon her.

One man, shirtless on his horse but wearing a broad-brimmed hat, whooped at her and grabbed for Daisy's bridle. "Look what we've got here this evening," he bellowed at the top of his lungs.

Clarinda took up her shotgun and pointed it at the man's chest, which was a moving target in the bright moonlight. "Meet your maker!" she cried and pumped in a shell, but as her finger tightened on the trigger there was a crack like a tree breaking and the weapon was torn from her hand. Another cowboy had used his bullwhip to disarm her, and she saw her prize gun fly through the air into the bushes. A rider leapt from his horse into the seat beside her and began wrestling her for the reins. That was with one hand. The other was trying to pull down her shirt.

Desperately she reached under the seat and got ahold of the bag Gawain had left her. While the cowhand had turned his attention to spreading her thighs, right there on the wagon's rough seat, she pulled open the bag and raised up her twisting red-striped snake.

As luck would have it, she had caught it midsection, so it thrashed madly from both ends and tried to bite her while she stuck it into her assailant's face. The man made an unpleasant sound and tumbled off the wagon into the road. Madly, Clarinda swung the snake around in arcs at the heads of the riders surrounding her, and the bunch backed off to decide what to do.

The standoff came to a sudden end when the cowboys' boss raced up; the deference the others showed him made his position clear. He rode his horse between Clarinda in her wagon and the three cowboys and pulled it to an abrupt stop.

"What's all this?" he demanded. Clarinda still had the snake, but it had bitten her wrist so she tossed it at the men. They backed off some more.

"These men attacked me," she cried and pointed her finger at them, like it had a witch's power to strike them dead.

"We'll have none of that," the boss said.

"Give me back my shotgun!" she insisted.

The boss looked over his shoulder, and one of the riders dismounted and recovered her weapon from the weeds. He handed it to the boss, who paused to examine it.

"Unusual gun," he said. "And now, Miss, what might you be doing out here on this road late on this particular evening?"

"That's none of your business, is it? Give me my shotgun and go on about you own." He was a nice looking man, she thought. A head of wavy blond hair, a square jaw, and a fancy mustache. He was dressed well, just as she imagined a rich rancher might look.

"I suppose it's not my business," the boss acknowledged, looking her up and down. "You're a nice looking lassie if I do say so, and you know how to take care of yourself. What's your name?"

"My name is Clarinda, and I'll thank you to hand over that firearm."

"Yes, ma'am," he said, and gave her a wink, she thought, but under his hat it was hard to tell. In the background, the cabin they had set afire collapsed, and she thought she heard someone scream.

"My name's Jasper Braxton," he told her, "and I look forward to meeting you again." He handed her the shotgun, stock first, and the riders behind him all instinctively put their hands on their holsters.

"Not very likely," she said, and snapped the reins. Her wagon rolled off, and all the men laughed. In a few minutes, the cabin fire had disappeared into the quiet woodlands.

She was sorry she had lost Gawain's snake. Her hand was swollen from its bites, but he had said it wasn't poisonous.

"Don't quite know where I am," she mumbled nonsense to Daisy, "But we're gonna get there."

But not as quickly as she thought. The road was not so easy as Gawain had predicted it would be, and before long it was pitch black and Clarinda was lost. She saw the light from a distant farmhouse way back in the prairie, but she preferred her chances, as a woman alone, by staying alone. But for the loneliness it was a pleasant night, the kind she loved, and, finding a small spring, she allowed Daisy to drink while she drifted off to sleep.

CHAPTER NINETEEN
MY NIGHT

Whistler and I had ridden quite a few miles toward Manatee City before the exhaustion of my recent exertions and the lateness of the day caught up with me. Somehow the urgency of reporting to the sheriff was less important now. The world had changed. I was in love.

I started thinking about finding a place to rest. As coincidence would have it, I came upon someone's camp. Off to the side of the road, beside a wagon and a tent, a fire was blazing. A horse neighed off in the trees and Whistler tossed his head and snorted.

"Howdy, stranger," a man's voice said, coming from near the tent.

"Howdy, yourself," I replied sociably. "Gettin' dark, ain't it." I jerked Whistler's reins and patted my horse's shoulder to calm him.

"It sure is. You just passing through?"

"I'm on my way to Manatee City," I told the man, whom I still couldn't quite see due to the shadows of the trees he was sitting under.

"Then you've got a ways to go. You're welcome to tarry and get a cup of coffee if you want."

"Much obliged," I said. "Would you mind stepping up so I can see who I'm talking to?"

The man got up and came forth, walking around the fire. He had a rifle resting on his shoulder.

"I think I know you," I said. "Weren't you on the road a few days ago with your dead mother?"

"That's right," the young man said – he could have been even younger than me - "We buried her yesterday. And you was looking for Charley Willard if I'm not mistaken."

"I was, and I caught him."

"You're not the law, are you?

"I am. I'm a Deputy Sheriff."

"You don't look old enough to be a deputy anything," he said.

"Well, I am. When I met you before you denied knowing Charley Willard. Are you a friend of his?" I kept a watchful eye on this fellow's gun.

"Not especially. Him and me trapped alligators together one time over on the Myakka River. He cheated me out of my money. Anyhow, you asked me had I seen him, which I hadn't."

"Then you may want to know that he's in the Pine Level jail for murder."

"Well, it wouldn't be a great loss to the world if ol' Charley got hung." He turned his back on me and went back to the stump he had been sitting on. "Coffee's here if you want some," he said.

"Guess I will," I said, and dismounted. "Any water here for my horse?"

"There's a spring over there under that tall cypress. You can introduce your horse to mine."

As we settled down and conversed, I learned that the man's name was Rusty Wade, and that he was setting up to be a fishing guide on Lemon Bay in a new town they planned to call Grove City, just as soon as it was built. There was not much future in alligator trapping, he had decided. The real money would be in Yankee tourists.

"Where did you go," I inquired, "when you were driving around your dead mother, if you don't mind me asking."

"Quite some distance. There were a number of places she always liked and wished to see again if she hadn't got so sick. There was a little church up in Fort Crawford where she and my dad got married. And a cedar grove on Joshua Creek where I was led to believe I got conceived. And we went to a place they call Mangrove Point, which my mother always said had the prettiest view of the ocean she'd ever seen. 'Course, it turns out that it looks over Charlotte Harbor, which is big but not actually the ocean. Anyway, that's the trip we took together."

"I don't know where those places are," I admitted, "but I can see you've been on a long road, just like me."

"I've seen some things, and..." Wade's hand went to the rifle beside him. "Someone's coming," he said.

We could hear the horse's hooves clopping slowly down the road and set aside our coffee cups to wait for whatever appeared.

The horse stopped when it was still a shadow in the trees.

"Hello, the camp," a gravelly voice called.

"Is that Captain Duff?" I shouted in astonishment. I had feared the

Captain was dead.

The rider kicked his horse forward. "Young Gawain," he said happily.

"Friend of yours?" Wade whispered.

"You bet," I said, hastening to my feet to greet the Captain.

I helped him off his horse.

"I've had a merry chase finding you, boy," the Captain said. "I've got to say I'm a little stiff. You got anything to eat or coffee?"

"Sure," I told him. I was happier than a preacher at a church picnic. I introduced the Captain to Rusty Wade. "I first met Rusty when I was tracking Willard," I explained. "He was riding his mother around to some of the places she liked."

"That's nice," the Captain said. "I wish my mother was alive to take to her favorite places."

"Me, too," said Wade. His comment startled the Captain, but he was too weary to pursue it.

Wade rummaged in his pack and came up with some hard sausage. "I've got the makings for biscuits if you want to go to the trouble," he offered. "It won't be long till morning."

"That does sound inviting." The Captain sat down beside the fire. "But I think after I size this boy up, I might do with a little shut-eye. It's been a long, long ride."

They passed around the coffee pot one more time, while I talked about catching Willard in the Blackjack, a place unknown to the older man. Wade just listened.

Finally, I noticed the bulge in the Captain's shirt, and realized that it covered up bandages.

"Lord, Captain, you're still mending. You'd better get some sleep."

The Captain laughed and coughed, tipped over backwards to rest his shoulders on the ground, and immediately began to snore under a blanket of stars.

"That's it for him," Wade observed. "I guess I'll lay down for an hour or two myself."

Left with no one to talk to, I tended to Captain Duff's horse, then bunked down on the soft earth with my saddle for a pillow and pulled my hat over his eyes. There was a smile on my face when I fell asleep.

RUSTY WADE'S STORY

Not everyone understands a mother's love. Or loyalty. My family was in a gang. Well, we were the gang. We robbed a bank in Leon County. That was just the start of it. Frank, my dad, got wounded running out the door and that slowed us way down. The sheriff up there didn't have any trouble tracking us, and my brother Norby had to shoot him off his horse. So then we were on the run for murder with dad bleeding all over the place. Norby and my sister Ada wanted to leave us behind and get away, but Ma said no to that. Norby and Ada made a run for it anyway, and tried to take the bank loot with them. Ma grabbed a burning stick from our campfire and swung it right in their horses' faces. I remember this very well. She shot her daughter in the foot, and my sister dropped the bag of cash, but they both rode off.

That left us with Dad, and we got him to a country doctor who was our distant kin. But he couldn't do a thing for him. Daddy was too far gone, and he died. This doctor didn't want his body around, naturally, so me and Ma had to carry him quite a ways before we found a preacher who didn't know about any bank robbery or shooting and was pleased to plant him in a little cemetery he had there near Alachua for a modest donation to his church. It was nice enough there, so we settled down in a rented farmhouse. There was talk of me going to school. I was fourteen.

Ma looked after me, and I looked after her. I won't say how we made our living, but it wasn't a picnic in the park. I learned a trade or two. Carpentry, fishing, gator hunting, and some house thievery here and there. That got me into some trouble, and though nobody could prove it was me, the local law decided to lock me up. We got the word in time, and Ma packed us up and we rode, leaving everything in the house behind.

I guess I could have survived until early manhood without my mother's guidance and care, but I'm glad I didn't have to try. She raised me right, and we put down our roots near Horse Creek in the southern part of Manatee County. I gave up my criminal inclinations because it wasn't necessary. There wasn't nothing to steal, there was nobody chasing us, and there were people around who was just glad to have neighbors and who shared what little they had until we could get in a garden of our own.

I turned out all right. I can do a day's work, and I will prosper here in South Florida one way or the other. It's going to be hard to find a woman as decent as my Ma to be the mother of my own kids, if ever I may have them.

Rusty Wade made his frying-pan biscuits the next morning and had boiled a pot of coffee by the time Captain Duff and I had our eyes open. The Captain wandered over to the spring to splash water in his face and do his business. He apologized for "oversleeping" when he got back.

Wade said not to worry. Anyway, he said, he was satisfied with his campsite and thought he would stay another day.

"Enjoy your mother while you have the time with her," Duff advised as he mounted up. "Life is too short."

"That's my attitude as well," Wade told him. "Y'all have a safe ride. There's some crazy fools in this county."

I rode off with the Captain, pointed north to Manatee City.

I was anxious to share what Charley Willard had divulged to me about the Abbe murder. "Willard said it was Bidwell, Bacon, Anderson and Andrews, all in a gang. There were some others, too. Bidwell and Andrews were in charge. They was out to kill Republican carpetbaggers, and Mister Abbe was the number one on the list. Actually, he was the number two because they had already killed another man named Riley last summer on the new road over to Sarasota."

"Is that the farmer we heard some talk about? There was never any report made to the sheriff," the Captain said.

"No, sir. It was kept quiet. But there was a whole list of men that was to get killed. They called themselves the Sarasota Vigilance Society, and it was all secret, with oaths and handshakes and everything!"

"I thought the War was supposed to be over. Willard told you all this?"

"Yes, sir. He did."

"Why?"

"He wants mercy and to avoid the hangman. And maybe he was afraid I'd kill him if he didn't."

"Reason I ask," Duff said, "is he denied everything to me over at the jail. Seems like he has had a change of heart."

I absorbed that news quietly as our horses trotted steadily along. After a minute of silence, he continued, "Now, tell me about this girl who you joined up with. What's her name?"

"Clarinda Barlow," I said, snapping out of it. "She's pretty and can take care of herself more'n any woman I ever knew."

Duff suppressed a laugh. "That's all good and fine," he said. "Why'd you let her go off by herself on a long night's ride to Sarasota?"

"She wouldn't have it any other way. She definitely knows her mind."

This time Duff did laugh, and it hurt his chest. "You just described my wife, Ellen, son. It worked for me so maybe it will work for you."

"I don't know. We haven't done anything," I lied, "except kiss."

"And capture an outlaw together," Duff pointed out.

I nodded. "I just don't know if I'm ready to settle down."

"Of course you're not. You're a young man." He held up his hand to stop me from saying what he knew was coming. "Yes, yes. I know. I joined up with the Alabama cavalry when I was almost as wet behind the ears as you, but this ain't no war."

"Captain Duff," I said with determination. "I feel like I've been in a war these past ten days. It wasn't any Sunday school party where I went. I handled Indians and crackers, and I crawled into the Blackjack to drag out that poor excuse of a man just to save his life so he could hang, and I did what was my duty, so I don't think there should be any doubt about me being old enough to get on take care of my own affairs now."

"Damn!" Duff said. "Maybe you'll make a lawyer." His jest was to cover up the wetness of his eyes. "No more argument from me. Next one you got to straighten out is your...the sheriff." Duff clamped his jaw shut.

CHAPTER TWENTY

MANATEE CITY—AND
THE SHERIFF GETS US ORGANIZED

The sheriff was at his small office in the old courthouse, the one used before the county seat had been moved further inland to Pine Level. The town was thriving on the river trade and tourism, but Sheriff Watson's office wasn't much besides a desk, a stove, and a gun rack. It was usually empty because he thought it safer to keep his firearms at home. A gentle rain fell on the town, carried on a slow breeze, and that plus the distant thunder probably explained why Sheriff Watson had his eyes closed, his feet up and his chair tilted back.

He came awake as soon as I barged through the door. "You're back," he practically shouted. "Good God!"

"Yes, sir. And I caught Charley Willard!" Watson couldn't help but see that I had a slight swagger..

I explained what had happened after Captain Duff was shot, the difficulty of trailing the murderer, the Indians, the river crossings, and the trials of the Blackjack. I told about all the help given me by Clarinda Barlow.

Sheriff Watson started to raise a question, but I kept going, describing in detail what Willard had told me about the Abbe shooting.

The sheriff rubbed his chin while he thought that over. "Seems like you've taken this law enforcement business very seriously. Maybe too seriously for a fellow your age."

"Like you once told me, sir, ..."

"I know," Sheriff Watson said. "Anyway, Willard's explanation don't make complete sense. Abbe was a Republican, sure enough, and he didn't hide the fact. But he's been a good citizen down here for more than ten years, and he's the U. S. Commissioner. He's supported my election, and it's well known that I'm a Democrat. I've heard him say lots of things against the Reconstruction government we've had to put up with till now. And as for Bidwell, his own brother was a Union Army general, and I guess that don't exactly make him a Florida cracker!"

"All of that may be true, but I'm telling you what Willard confessed to me. If Bidwell was spinning a yarn, Charley believed it and joined in the killing spree. That bunch is going to kill more if they aren't stopped. Willard bared his soul to me."

"Bared it, did he? You must have put the fear of God in him."

"I reckon I did! The fear of the Devil. He told me Bidwell and Andrews were the men behind all of this, the heads of their gang. And once you took their oath, if anybody backed out of a killing, the others were sworn to kill the one who was chicken."

"You think Willard will repeat any of this in court?"

"Don't know if he will or not, but we got an eye witness says he pulled the trigger on Abbe. Everybody heard the shotgun go off twice, and said it was Anderson's gun. Plus, Willard shot Captain Duff off his horse in cold blood with witnesses right there. Willard is bound to hang if he doesn't tell the truth, and he's got to be scared of having a noose around his own neck. Clarinda Barlow heard his confession, too."

The sheriff reflected a minute, then said, "That's quite a story, Gawain. I guess we better go and round up these men before they carry out any more of their wicked plans. And I've got to see a judge." Having decided that, he moved fast to pack up ammunition, and he dispatched me into town to try to round up another deputy or two.

On the way out the door, I had to inquire, "Is there any reward for bringing Willard in?"

"Hadn't thought about it," the sheriff said. "Why?"

"I owe the man at the river who give me his wagon."

"We'll tend to that later. Git!"

It was still well before noon. Captain Duff had ridden to his house a mile from town to show his wife Ellen that he was okay. He tarried long enough to let her change the dressing on his shoulder and then attempted to hurry to join the sheriff's fresh posse. He failed to reckon, however, with his wife. She put her foot down, told him he had reached the end of his tether and her patience, and got him back to bed.

Sheriff Watson and me and the other men rounded up for the posse, upholding the long arm of the law, rode hard for fifteen miles down the dirt road to Sarasota.

First, we all broke open the door to Ed Bacon's beach shanty, the palm covered shack his father owned, and held him at gunpoint while we pulled off his shoes. "You got the wrong man!" Bacon protested, but his unusually narrow left foot told the tale. He was handcuffed and shoved onto a horse.

We barged through the door where Adam Hunter lived – the man called "Doctor" who clerked at Bidwell's store. The sheriff stopped short when he saw who Hunter had for company. It was a prominent local land developer.

The unexpected interloper, I knew, was named Jasper Braxton, and he had lived in Manatee City for the past few years. He was a man on the rise to hear people talk. He had blond hair, the flair of a handsome man, and a wavy waxed mustache. I remembered selling him several crates of oranges. They were to be shipped by fast train to an address on Chestnut Street in Boston, and I had made the arrangements for delivery to the railhead at Cedar Key. That transaction had stuck in my head.

"What are you doing here, Jasper?" the sheriff asked, surprised.

"Hello, Sheriff. I'm here on business. Looks like you are, too."

"What kind of business would that be?" the sheriff asked, suspicious.

Dr. Hunter, the wanted man, had rocked back in his chair as if to distance himself from this conversation. He was small, dark and nervous. I took a step closer to an open window to prevent any sudden exits.

"You know me, Sheriff," Braxton said easily. "I buy and sell land for a living, and Hunter and I were discussing some property he might want to sell."

"Is that right, Hunter?" Watson asked. "Are you maybe thinking about selling this place and moving on?"

"That's my private affair," Hunter said, his first words since the law had kicked open his front door and made ourselves at home.

"Well, I sure hate to interrupt your private affairs, but I got a warrant for your arrest."

Over his loud objections, we scooped up Dr. Hunter, escorted him outside and put him on the same horse with Ed Bacon.

Jasper Braxton followed the party outside and mounted his own horse. "Seems I wasted a trip down here. I'll see you back in town, Sheriff." He tipped his hat and took note of me – I admit I did look like a man to be reckoned with and I was giving him a glare to show I didn't believe a word he said. He rode away without a backwards look.

"Mister Braxton sure gets around," I said.

"Don't he though," the sheriff muttered. "Give him time and he'll own all of Manatee County. But we best forget about him and get on with it," he said, giving the reins a snap.

On his way out of Sarasota, Jasper Braxton was surprised to come upon Clarinda in her wagon. She was slowly navigating the unfamiliar streets in search of Gawain. Braxton jerked his horse to a halt next to her and gave her a big smile.

"You look mighty nice in the daytime, 'Miss Shotgun'," he said.

"Mind your sass," she replied and cracked the reins. But deep down, she was pleased. Very pleased.

The posse next burst into Bidwell's store where a customer was paying for a jar of Tupelo Honey. Bidwell took one look and grabbed a pill bottle from the shelf behind him. He tipped it to his lips and gobbled down all he could before the sheriff slapped the bottle out of his hand.

I rushed forward to get the handcuffs on him, and the sheriff picked the bottle off the floor.

"Morphine," he grumbled. "We may be taking a dead man to jail." Bidwell collapsed to his knees. We dragged our captive outside where we fortunately found the store's delivery wagon. Its side was decorated with a painted ad for "Bidwell's Convenient Store." The sheriff and

I loaded its collapsed owner in the back and packed Bacon and Dr. Hunter in with him.

We had just mounted our horses when Clarinda clattered up in her rig. The posse took a quick breather while I excitedly introduced the sheriff and Clarinda to one another.

She said she was glad to meet him, and he said the same to her, but then the sheriff motioned me aside. "Don't you get serious about that girl. You're too young for that, and she don't look to be more'n fourteen."

"She's old enough," I said. "And she's got spunk."

The sheriff frowned and shook his head. "I guess we'll be heading out now," he said. "We've got Dr. Andrews to find over on Bee Ridge." To his men he yelled, "Let's ride!"

Before they could take off, I quietly told him, "I'd kind of like to pay my respects to Mrs. Abbe, and tell her we got the man who shot her husband."

"I think that's a very good idea, son. You ran the son of a bitch down, so it's your place to give her the news. Let her know I'll be by myself just soon as I get all these boys locked up. They've got friends around here who might have an idea about ambushing us and settin' them all free. Word's already out around the county, I reckon, and we best get them over to Pine Level without any more delay. Now, I'm telling you, be careful around that girl!"

"Sure," I said under my breath, thinking it was a little late for the sheriff to be so protective of my welfare. Could it be because Mrs. Watson was no longer around? Or did he care for me more since I had brought in a criminal? I had never felt resentful about my situation before. But maybe being unhappy about the way you were raised is a part of growing up.

The posse and the wagonload of prisoners set off, disappearing quickly into the dust clouds they stirred up on the road.

ED BACON'S STORY

I don't have any story. And if I did, why would I tell it to you?

Clarinda came with me to the Abbe home on its shady lane. I knocked on the front door. A young woman in a pressed black dress answered and took us into the drawing room where Mrs. Abbe, also wearing mourning clothes, was seated with her Illinois friend, Mr. Morehouse. I had already heard Morehouse's eye-witness account of the murder - on the very day of Abbe's death.

Mrs. Abbe gave me an inquisitive look.

"I'm the one who caught that killer Willard and brought him in," I said to explain myself. "This here is Clarinda Barlow. She helped me get the man into the Pine Level jail, which wasn't easy."

"I'm happy to meet you. Have a seat, please," the widow said. "You look like you could use some food in you."

"Yes, ma'am, but I came here to say how sorry I was and to assure you that justice is being carried out."

"That's very well put, young man. Sounded like my Charles, the way you said that. And you, young lady, you look plumb wore out."

"I'm all right," Clarinda said, embarrassed at how she must look in such a nice house.

"Of course you are. Mister Morehouse, please take this young man into the kitchen and see if there's not some crackers and cheese or some boiled eggs he might eat to hold his ribs together. Clarinda, you come with me."

Within half an hour I got some nourishment and Clarinda got a clean dress and a blue pin for her blond hair.

We all sat down together in the front room and I repeated the story of the pursuit, the capture, and the dangerous trip to the jail. I also added a report of the multiple arrests on this very exciting day.

"Did you say Jasper Braxton was at the Hunter house when the sheriff got there?" Mrs. Abbe inquired.

"Yes, ma'am."

"My husband and that man Jasper Braxton didn't get along. He was trying to talk Charles into selling some of our property right here along Sarasota Bay. He wanted it for a hotel because he said the railroads would be soon coming through. But Charles wasn't interested."

"No ma'am?"

"What Charles said to me was, yes, the railroad was going to come, but the Abbes could run their own hotel. That was one of his dreams, and I don't suppose he was willing to lose it, even though, as he told me, the money Braxton offered was good."

"How'd that go over with Jasper Braxton?"

"I don't guess it went over too well, but Charles never brought it up again, and I didn't question him about it."

"I'd bet you could still sell if you wanted the money," Clarinda piped up, and then looked down at her hands.

"No, dear. I'm going to stay right here. This is where my children live. Mister Morehouse will help me go through all the books, and I have faith that we'll get by. You've had to struggle yourself, have you honey?"

"Yes, I have," Clarinda said proudly, "and I ain't been knocked down yet." And that was when I, looking back later, would say if asked that I became certain she was the one for me.

"Neither have I," Mrs. Abbe said, smiling for the first time. "And I hope to take my husband's position and be the first woman postmaster in Southwest Florida."

Clarinda laughed and clapped, which seemed out of place in a house of grieving but Mrs. Abbe liked it.

"Where do you call home?" she asked.

"I live with my pa down in the south part of the county about a day and a half's ride from here so long as it doesn't rain and muck up the roads and flood the creeks."

"Where do you plan to spend the night, dear?"

"I hadn't thought about it." Clarinda looked sideways at me.

"I'll just built me a fire down at the water where the bugs ain't bad and camp out," I told Mrs. Abbe.

"Fine for you, Gawain," the widow exclaimed, "but not for you, young lady. You can sleep here at this house."

"I couldn't," Clarinda protested.

"You will, too. And you can help me fix supper."

And that's the way it happened. It was a good meal, with mashed potatoes and smoked pork and tomatoes and greens from the garden. And when it was done, I said goodnight and led Whistler down to the beach to make my camp. The spot I picked was very near where Captain Duff, Sheriff Watson, and me had slept the night after Abbe was killed.

I thought back to that evening as I lay down alone beside my campfire. It was the night I had received the book of poems and the twenty-dollar gold piece left me by my father. I never did know of any other possessions my father might have had, except that photograph of my mother. As a boy I'd been told that the old MacFarlane house where I was born had burned down. I had always assumed that the fire occurred after my father died, but then again, maybe the fire was the cause of his death. Or maybe my father had caused the fire and then died in it. There were a lot of details that needed to be filled in.

I supposed that Sheriff Watson should have given me those facts, or I should have asked more questions. Perhaps my ignorance was due to my somewhat isolated upbringing out on the Watson country acres, where the sum of my companions, other than Reuben, were the Ephrams and their offspring. None of those souls had first-hand knowledge of my ancestry, or so they claimed.

But now I was consumed by curiosity. In the past Sheriff Watson had always had a way of deflecting questions, or maybe it was rounding the edges off the answers, so that only a minimum of information actually slipped through. Captain Duff had seemed about ready to fill in some of the gaps when we were on the trail, before the bastard Willard shot him. Perhaps the sherriff would be more forthcoming now.

The stars were out in full and the air was just a little chilly. A breeze off the Gulf kept the fire popping and the no-see-ums at bay. Instead of welcoming sleep, however, my mind hopped around from one thing to another. There was the dull, violent, stupidity I'd seen in Willard's eyes when he had Clarinda in his grip. There was the foul smell about him. There was his willingness to give up his accomplices in the Vigilance Society, the Vigilante Society, or the Assassination Society, whatever you wanted to call it. Just for the pathetic hope of saving his own skin.

Thoughts of Clarinda was a balm to those images. She was way past pretty to me now. The vision of her standing naked by the creek was burned forever in my mind. Nothing had ever compared to the softness of her skin, and her soft touch on mine. Not that she wasn't strong. She was strong and soft.

She would be hard to tame, and wasn't that what a man was supposed to do with a woman? But laying with her had been better than any dream, and remembering it, the closeness of her body, stirred me deeply and crowded out good sense. Taming her was the last thing I had in mind.

I had known how men and women made love, sort of. I'd seen that couple twisting about in the lemon grove, and of course I'd seen cows and horses, dogs and pigs do it. Nobody had explained to me whether it was a good thing or a bad thing, or when a man was supposed to do it and when he wasn't. But now I had done it, and it didn't feel bad at all. I hadn't forced my affections on Clarinda. In fact, she had seemed to be way ahead of me in that department. I wondered what the next step for us would be. What kind of life would she have if she returned home to be with Pa Barlow?

I closed my eyes to concentrate on bringing to mind her physical assets, which are unquestionably impressive, but my pleasant reverie was abruptly cut short by a bonfire flaring up down the beach. It was right beneath Bidwell's dock. There was quite a blaze so I cast my fantasies aside and jumped up to get closer and see what might be happening.

Two men, silhouetted by the flames, were feeding the flames, but it didn't look to be logs they were tossing on. Keeping to the shadows, I walked a little further. The men were burning papers.

"Hey!" I shouted. "What are you boys doing?"

"None of your business," one of the men yelled, surprised at the intrusion.

"Don't know about that," I said and walked into the light. The man who had spoken was Jasper Braxton, the real estate broker.

"Who are you anyway?" the other one asked. He was dark-haired, short and solid, and was wearing a black suit. I recognized him right away.

"I know who you are," I said. "You're William Bartholomew, the lawyer Willard went to for help when he was on the run."

"I remember you now," Bartholomew said. "You were along with that posse who rode onto my place accusing me of something. You're just a boy."

"I'm a Deputy Sheriff," I informed him. "Now what is it you gents are burning out here in front of Bidwell's store? I guess you know we arrested him this morning."

Braxton tossed a whole box of papers into the fire while this exchange was going on.

"Hey, stop that!" I protested.

"Have you got some kind of a warrant?" the lawyer demanded. "People have a right to dispose of trash on a public beach."

I was uncertain of my powers in this situation. Braxton fed more documents into the flames but said, by way of keeping the conversation going, "You certainly have a lot of balls for a man your age. I could use someone like you in my operation."

"Doing what?"

"Riding the range. Keeping squatters off my properties." All the while, he kept feeding the fire.

"I'm going to find out what right you have to be here," I said and climbed the ladder onto the Bidwell dock. I ran around to the front of the store to beat on the door. Nobody answered, but there was a lantern burning in the house adjacent, which I knew to be the Dr. Hunter's.

"What do you want?" a little child's voice called out the window.

"I want to speak to your mother."

I heard the child calling for his mother, and in a moment a woman stuck her head out of the window and asked again who I was. I told her. "I'm a deputy sheriff, and there's men down by the water burning papers. I want to know if they have permission to do so."

"You're the people who arrested my husband!" the woman shouted, "and you can get your dirty old selves out of here and quit bothering decent women and children in the dead of night!"

"Yes ma'am, but…"

She slammed the shutters in my face. Just then I heard the sound of horses' hooves pounding off down the road. I raced back to the beach to find the fire dying down. The wind whipped fragments of paper around in tiny tornadoes. Bartholomew and Braxton had cleared out.

I grabbed helplessly at the bits of paper in the air. Seeing some sheets blowing down the beach, I chased after them and was able to save a few pages from the surf. I took these back to my own camp and smoothed them out.

One appeared to be a printed program for a social event at:

THE BOSTON CLUB

JACKSONVILLE, FLORIDA

There was a description of a Saturday evening "soiree" featuring the "Hambone Minstrel Show." This meant nothing to me, except that I'd once shipped Mr. Braxton's oranges to an address in Boston.

Another was a handwritten sheet, with the page number "11" at the bottom, which was titled, "Secret Handshake." There was an illustration of two hands gripped together in a manner described as:

"Take hold of the other man's hand like an ordinary handshake, but left-handed, and press your thumb in between the second and third knuckles. If a friend, he will respond in kind."

The third was a legal document, also handwritten but elegantly, styled, "Quitclaim Deed," and it referenced a man named Creed Driggers passing title of some property to a company called "Great State Development Company." I had a little knowledge about what a quitclaim deed was. It was what you got from a squatter if you wanted his land.

The fourth was the fragment of a letter. At the top of the page was an engraved heading, "The Florida Mortgage and Investment Company, Limited, Edinburgh." It was addressed to "The Hon. Alfred Bidwell," and it began, "Dear Mr. Bidwell. Allow me to introduce our agent..." The rest of the letter was burned away.

CHAPTER TWENTY-ONE

MY CONVERSATION

After a pleasant but late breakfast presented by Mrs. Abbe, I set out alone for Manatee City. Clarinda stayed behind at the Abbe house, where she had become welcome company to the widow. On reaching the county seat, my first order of business was to tell the sheriff about the men on the beach and give the him the documents I had found.

Sheriff Watson looked them over, then invited me to join him for a walk around downtown. We ended up sitting on the town's main dock overlooking the river.

"I have to tell you I'm mighty proud of the way you brought that man Willard in," the sheriff said.

"Thank you, sir. It weren't easy."

"I know it wasn't, especially after all the other deputies left you out there in the scrub alone."

"I don't really blame them. I did at the time, but I understand now they all have wives and families, and seein' Captain Duff shot like that could knock the sand out of anybody."

"Anybody, sure, but not you," he said proudly. "You know what one of them boys told me yesterday? He said they may not have actually caught Willard themselves, but by running him ragged across half the state they 'supplied the means' for his capture." The sheriff laughed.

I brushed an ant off my boot and it disappeared down a crack between two dock boards. "I didn't kill that ant," I said. "I just supplied the means for it to drown. Or it might just float away and live a long and happy life as a free ant in Key West."

The sheriff chuckled. "Them papers you found are mighty interesting," he said. "I'll ask at the land broker's office, but I can see that the property in question is in a homestead area. This "Great State" concern has likely filed a claim for it, and I imagine that man Driggers is a farmer they want off the land. They probably paid him a few dollars to give up his squatters' rights or else got him drunk enough to sign the paper. What do you think I ought to do with that document?"

"You mean it's not recorded."

"Don't appear to be. You brought in the original."

"Burn it," I said firmly.

"Can't do that. There are certain rules you got to follow with evidence. I think I'll just keep it in the safe for the time being. And another thing, I don't know exactly how you convinced Willard to spill his guts, but I do have to ask him, and should he say that you tortured it out of him, would you call him a liar?"

"Everybody knows that Willard's a liar," I said. "It won't damage his reputation none if one more person says it."

"Then that's the way it is. We'll have to see how this plays out. What do you plan to do with yourself now? I can't pay you much to be a deputy, and some people would say I'm favoring my family if I did hire you permanently."

"Mister Braxton offered me a job."

"Was that before or after you interrupted him burning those papers."

"Sort of in the middle of it."

"A job doing what?"

"I guess riding around whatever land he owns and looking after things."

"Do you know what the Florida Mortgage and Investment Company is?"

"The company that wrote the letter to Alfred Bidwell? First I ever heard of it."

"I can tell you that they are interested in buying up a whole lot of land in South County, around Sarasota. It's supposed to be a world-class outfit."

"I wonder what their business is with Bidwell, and who their agent is."

Sheriff Watson nodded and looked over the water. "I guess we'll find out in good time," he said.

That seemed to me to be a less than dynamic approach to the investigation, but the sheriff had something else on his mind.

"Are you thinking about marrying that girl?" he asked.

I was embarrassed. "I don't know. I sort of just met her."

"My advice would be to take your time, son."

I studied the sheriff's profile and decided, since we were talking man-to-man, to take a chance. "There's something I've been wondering about," I said. "How did my father ever, you know, make a baby, make me, with half his innards blowed out?"

My guardian jumped up. "Sweet Jesus, Gawain! Where do you get a question like that? I know they did whatever they could do, and your father wanted a child, a son. And you're what he got! Now maybe you do need to find work somewhere's else where your past won't worry you so much."

I recoiled in shock. "Are you telling me I can't ask questions about my own family?"

The sheriff shook his head, turned and walked off the dock.

Was I angry about being dismissed in that way? You bet! But I followed him back to the jail, and he had a surprise for me. It developed that there was a reward for capturing Charley Willard. Fifty dollars. Sheriff Watson paid it over to me without saying another word about our conversation, and I left him that way.

A week went by and Captain Duff's wife and daughters were ready for him to be "de-commissioned" as a deputy for many reasons, like his health, his business, and the pleasure of his company. And, they argued, it would be no problem for Sheriff Watson to let him go. But Duff went to talk to the sheriff about it anyway.

"Seems to me, all the shooting's over," Duff told his friend. "I'd give you back my badge, but I think your boy still wears it."

"Go home to your wife," the sheriff told him. "I'll be sure you are paid for all your time, eventually."

"That's fine, no hurry. And Gawain, too?"

"My office has a small budget, but I can't say he doesn't deserve his pay, too."

"That, and a lot more. Gawain is a fine young man. You might want to give him more of your attention. He'd provide you with a lot of help."

"I don't know about that, Duff. He's got a job to do on my farm, and I don't see any reason to change anything."

The Captain stood up, laid his right hand on the sheriff's shoulder and tightened his grip so there would be no ignoring it. "Sandy, you're thinking about your budget, and public safety, and subduing all the miscreants in this county, and what you should be thinking about is that young man. He's somebody to be proud of, to bring along."

"Hell, I know that. I am proud of him."

"No, man. That's not it. You should tell him who his father is."

The sheriff's face froze. "I've got five other kids to think about. My wife, bless her soul, isn't here to help me. You've said enough. Now, you get out and let's leave it this way, parting as friends."

"I guess that's why you let him get half-raised by the Ephrams," said the Captain, backing up. "But I think the world of that boy. If you don't want him, I'm going to offer him a job with me."

CHAPTER TWENTY-TWO

STARTING OUR LIVES

Now I had tangled with killers, but I wasn't very wise in the ways of the world. I thought I could wrestle life any way I wished because I was strong and tough. I thought I could run a farm, because I wanted to, and could make a living at it, because I wanted to. Dangers and pitfalls were nowhere in my line of view. I thought I was the man in charge, even when it came to Clarinda.

Clarinda, on the other hand, actually was quite wise about certain things. She might have had very little education in life's finer arts, but she knew exactly how rough a person's existence could get. She knew hunger, and she knew cold, and she knew all about being poor. What I came to find out was that what she wanted was a strong man, property with a good title (preferably close to town), and most of all, she wanted security. All I offered was the first of those. She must have decided I had good potential, however, and that, with her guidance, I could fill her cup the rest of the way up. So no matter what I might envision, we were going to get married, and soon. We had a long talk, and contrary to the sheriff's advice, decided to hitch up.

A colored preacher out in the country did the job for us. He was a brother-in-law of Hiram Ephram, who had raised me up. Clarinda wore the white dress her mother had made, the dress she wooed me in. I got excited just seeing it on her again. The ceremony was proceeding just fine until I noticed a small framed portrait hanging on the wall of the little church.

It was Zechariah, the crazy heathen from the Blackjack!

"What's he doing here?" I demanded.

"That's our founder, Reverend Caleb Dawes," the preacher said solemnly.

"His real name is Dawes, and he founded this church?" I was astonished.

"Indeed. He was quite a remarkable man. Saved many a soul before he left us."

"He surely did leave you!" I exclaimed, picturing the shroud-cloaked Zechariah crouched in the dusk of the Blackjack.

"Yes. He went out West, I think. On a pilgrimage."

I started to set this preacher straight about the destination of Zechariah's pilgrimage. It was to the Blackjack, not to California, but Clarinda was impatient to get this wedding business finished, so I left it alone.

After our brief ceremony, Clarinda and I headed back to my home in the barn. I felt bad that it was the best place I had to offer her, but she didn't seem to mind. She said she was already working on some other ideas. That was just like the Clarinda I would come to know over all the future years we were to spend together.

I have to admit that I was feeling a bit nervous on that ride to our home. I was, of course, looking forward to our first night together since the one we'd spent camped out in the woods. But things had just sort of happened that night – neither one of us had planned it or even thought it was possible. Now we were legally husband and wife, and I wasn't too sure how we were supposed to reach that same outcome – namely, Clarinda and me intertwined in what I guess you'd call a state of ecstasy.

Clarinda was unusually quiet on the ride home. Maybe she was thinking about the same thing.

As it turned out, I need not have worried. While I was somewhat clumsily lighting a fire to cook the pork chops and potatoes I'd bought as a celebration, Clarinda started sipping on the bottle of hard cider that Ruben had procured for me (having failed to find a bottle of real wine). I had a few slugs of it myself and before you know it, the two of us were laughing and carrying on about the events of the day. The pork chops were a big hit, and after dinner Clarinda got the urge to dance around the fire. I don't know what music she was hearing, but I sure did not mind the dance. She looked beautiful swaying in that same white dress she wearing that first night.

I could have watched her dance all night but she gradually wound down, drifting slowly by me, letting her hands trail through my hair and touch my face as she passed. It didn't take much of that treatment for me to know exactly where I wanted to be – where I wanted both of us to be. I stood up and kicked out the fire and as she floated close by, I swept her up in my arms and carried her straight to pallet I had fixed up as our bed in the barn.

She whispered my name as I lay her down as gently as I could. I felt like I should say something, something meaningful as this was the beginning of our married life. All I could think to do was say, "I love you, Clarinda. And I'm going to be the best husband to you that ever I can be." She smiled then and reached up for me. I didn't take much persuading.

The night will be forever in my mind. When I lifted her dress off, her breasts were even more perfect than I remembered. I bent over her and kissed her nipples as softly as I could, but that seemed to light a fire in her and she pulled my face down and moaned loudly when I sucked hard, maybe even nibbling her a little. In no time, I was out of my clothes and could feel the length of her body stretched out against mine. Her skin felt like I imagined silk might feel, and the place between her legs was so wet and warm and softly swollen; she bit my shoulder hard when I touched her there.

She wrapped her legs around me and held on tight as we danced together the first time and then over and over that night, with only the moonlight a witness to the joys two lovers can share.

Our lives together were not always perfect and maybe I did not always keep the promise I made to her that night. But still, when I lie dying, it's the memories of that night that I want to depart this life with.

For a honeymoon, Clarinda and I decided to go visiting and camping. In preparation for the trip we loaded our wagon up with plenty of food and tools and what plants, seeds and cuttings I could liberate from the Watson farm. We rode first into Sarasota, planning to picnic at the beach and visit with Mrs. Abbe. As we got closer to town, we passed other wagons, several carrying large family groups out for church or visiting relatives. At the approach of one wagon, Clarinda sat up to study the man and woman riding past us. The man had a heavy beard and was wearing a blue scarf over his forehead. The woman was attractive enough, but what I noticed was her fancy hat decorated with egret feathers. The couple stared straight ahead; they did not wave or say hello.

After they rode on Clarinda said, "That was my mother."

It was at that moment I guess, that she realized her mother would never be in her life again. Instead of crying about it she hid her feelings with a laugh. I tried to ask her questions, but it was something she didn't want to talk about. She did, however, want to see her father again and tell him about our wedding.

LOVELADY BARLOW'S STORY

Pa and Clarinda were occupied working by our cabin. I met the stranger in the woods, simple as that. He was hunting turkeys, and I was looking for a lost pig. He had a nice way about him, and he was a good looking man, a lot younger than Pa. We set down to talk. I guess I shouldn't have done that. He had a funny accent, and explained that he was from Scotland. He was exploring the area, and said hunting turkeys was just the best way to do it. His clothes weren't fancy, but they didn't come from around here. The shotgun he was using said Parker Brothers along the barrel by the hammer, I notice things like that. It might have cost more than our whole farm was worth. He helped me find my pig and said he hoped he'd see me again sometime. He'd be hunting in these woods every day, he said, at least for the next week. So that didn't give me much time.

It was just a crazy thing I did for love. I had a dream and I left behind my daughter for that dream, and for that I might perish in Hell, if there is such a place. I have to believe she would understand my decision, bad as it might have been, and will take care of herself. But the dream with the Scot man didn't work out. Yet with him gone, I have been fortunate to meet another gentleman of some means, a farmer with good property, a widower with two young children to whom I have not yet been introduced. He seems like a nice enough sort. Strong, with a burly beard. He has helped me with my little expenses here in the town of Nokomis, where I am keeping a lady's household.

Clarinda and I decided to take an extended honeymoon through "South County" in the general direction of the Peace River. We could visit Clarinda's Pa, scout out property along the way, and I needed to pay for the wagon that I had requisitioned to transport Willard. After fulfilling my bargain, I would still have more than $35 in cash and a $20 gold piece. Good land, I had heard, could still be bought for a dollar or two an acre if you knew how to do the paperwork and claim it. Another object of the trip was, on the way back, we could conveniently pass by the property described in the Driggers' quitclaim deed that I'd seen the sheriff put in the safe.

It would take a leisurely two days to reach the Barlow homestead, and we could enjoy the ride and the "alone time." Camping under the stars was just fine with us despite the mosquito swarms around sunset. It was an unusually dry spring, which kept the bugs down, but the farms we passed looked parched. Nevertheless, we could see that there were more and more people coming every month, clearing more land.

Pa Barlow's cabin came into view. It was mostly unchanged from the way it had looked back in winter. He was out in his field, the one he was clearing when he nearly burnt down his house, bent over and hoeing the weeds out of a row of pole beans.

"Good God!" he exclaimed when he saw who was in the wagon. "The Prodigal Daughter returns! Glad to see you child!"

She ran over and hugged him. I suspected that for Clarinda the separation had been more painful than she had let on. There was no way not to miss the man who had struggled to feed her for seventeen years and no way not to feel guilty for the way she had left him.

"Gawain and I got married, Dad," she told him.

That made him step back. "Damn, you're just a lass," he said.

"I know what I want, Pa, and I know how to take it!" she fired off.

"Yeah," he agreed, rolling his eyes. He offered me his sweaty hand, and I shook it heartily.

"We brought you a load of stuff," I told the old man.

The supplies were gratefully accepted, and that night we all feasted on a meal of pancakes and cane syrup, eggs and bacon that Clarinda fixed up. I had brought along a few bottles of illegal package liquor, and Mr. Barlow was especially delighted about that.

We stayed for two days, helping to plant the seeds and seedlings we had brought. I showed Mr. Barlow the technique I had learned from Piney Reasoner for grafting prime orange strains onto the gnarly trees in the old man's small orchard, and I did some hard labor plowing up more ground to expand the Barlow grove.

We promised to return soon and then began the next leg of our journey, traveling further south to the Peace River crossing. The road got rougher and the people fewer as we went along.

We hailed for the ferry when we got to the ford. The fellow who ran the place was surprised as all get-out to see his wagon pulling up on the opposite shore. He poled his ferry right over.

"Why I'll be blessed. I never thought I'd see you again," he said, quite pleased at the prospect of payment.

"Here's the $15." I held out fifteen bank notes. "You want this or do you want your rig back?"

"That rig looks worn out to me," the man said. "It was a lot better when I gave it to you. I'll take the cash." He could tell a lie a lot better than me, so the deal was done.

He invited us to spend the night on his side of the river, but I declined. I well remembered the Willard sympathizers who were in this area, and I didn't want to get any closer to the Blackjack, a place I never wanted to see again. The solitude of woods and prairie, with Clarinda beside me of course, would suit me just fine.

I did, however, inquire about a Creed Driggers, and whether the ferryman might know where he lived.

"I know that old geezer," the operator said. "He pays his bills, but he don't pay for some of the chickens he eats. I know just where him and his wife live."

I got the directions and figured it wouldn't take much of a detour on the way home to get there. That night we camped on an oak hammock five miles from the Peace, on the banks of a small slough, and watched the stars. I even pulled out my book of poems. Clarinda got that special glow in her eyes when she listened to me read the strange words.

Wilt thou be my Dearie?
When sorrow wrings thy gentle heart.
O wilt thou let me cheer thee!
By the treasure of my soul,
That's the love I bear thee

I swear and vow that only thou
Shall ever be my Dearie!
Only thou I swear and vow,
Shall ever be my Dearie!

Lassie, say thou lo'es me;
Or, if thou wilt na be my ain,
O say na thou'lt refuse me!
If it winna, canna be,
Thou for thine may choose me,
Let me, lassie, quickly die,
Still trusting that thou lo'es me!
Lassie, let me quickly die,
Still trusting that thou lo'es me!

After I finished, she started to cry. I didn't know what to do except to hold her. Later on she told me that this was the night, after we were already married, that she knew she had made the right decision.

It wasn't easy, even with good directions, to find the Driggers' place. It was located at the end of a rutted path off the "main trail," which itself wasn't really much more than a gopher tortoise track itself. We approached the house in the heat of the day and were surprised to see a well-constructed residence rather than the shack we had been expecting. Two large hounds stopped us a hundred feet short of the front porch and held us at bay until a tall thin man, pulling up his suspenders, opened the door to see who we were.

"Mister Driggers?" I called.

"Who wants to know," he shouted back.

"I'm Gawain MacFarlane, and I came here to inquire about your property. I don't mean any harm."

"Harm or not, what do you want to know about my property? It's mine and I'll thank you to get off it."

"Yes, sir. I'm a Deputy Sheriff," I lied, since the sheriff had taken back his badge, "and I've seen your deed to something called the Great State Corporation. I just want to be sure it's all on the up and up."

"There's nothing on the up and up about that bunch of crooks. If I see any of them around here again I'll shoot them as sure as shit stinks."

"I'm no friend of theirs either!" I yelled. "I'm wondering if they're thieves. This lady here is my wife, and I'd appreciate it if you wouldn't cuss around her."

"Hmmm." Driggers considered it. "I guess you can come on in." He called off his dogs and when they were back on the porch I urged Whistler to pull the wagon into the yard. Driggers was as long and skinny as a rake handle. He wore a pointy felt hat that added another foot to his height. He had to take it off to clear the doorway as he followed us inside. Mr. Driggers explained that his wife and children were away for the week visiting cousins. They had a lot of cousins.

The story the man told confirmed my suspicions. The Driggers had settled on this property in 1866, right after "the Surrender," he said. They had about eighty acres, but it had never been surveyed until recently. It was somebody else's surveyor who started the job. Creed had caught him with his transit, "they call it," out in the scrub. When the man wouldn't say who he worked for, Driggers and his dogs ran him off. "In a hurry," he stated, looking like the memory gave him pleasure.

Then they started coming. First it was that Sarasota Postmaster, Charles Abbe. After him came the Great State man, Jasper Braxton, and two "gunslingers" for his company.

Ah, so Great State was a Braxton outfit! This was enlightening.

Driggers went on to say that both Abbe and Jasper Braxton wanted his land. It was part of some much bigger plan they each had. Other settlers in the area had also gotten visits from them.

"Were they working together?" Clarinda asked.

Driggers looked her way, not expecting the woman to take part in the conversation.

"Hell no, excuse me ma'am! They was fighting each other for what's mine. They said it didn't rightfully belong to me anyway, but at least the postmaster offered me a decent price. Braxton wanted to give me pennies. I told them both the same thing. They could kiss my cracker butt! I ain't goin' to sell!"

"So was that the end of it?" she asked.

"It sure was, lady. Abbe left nicely. He was more of the gentleman. I had to put a gun on Braxton and his thugs to run them off. That was about a year ago, and they ain't been back since."

"I've seen a quitclaim deed you signed," I told him. "It turns over your property to Braxton."

"You don't say, you goddam sheriff's deputy!" Driggers' face went red. "I ain't never signed any such thing. You or anybody else comes in here with a line of crap like that and I'll blow their fuckin' head off!"

"Whoa, partner," I said, putting up my hands. "It ain't me who wants your property. I'm just telling you what I saw. It might even be I can get that deed torn up or given back to you."

"For what?" Driggers asked suspiciously.

"For nothing. I'm not a friend of Jasper Braxton. But you just may have to tell your story in a court of law one day."

"Here's my court of law!" Driggers said, producing the pistol he was holding under the table, unbeknownst to me. Departure seemed like the best idea.

"If I see that deed again I'll see that it gets torn up," I promised. "In any case, you told me a lot I didn't know."

We took our leave.

"Geez. At least you didn't get us shot," Clarinda said as we rode off the property.

Later that summer Clarinda and I found a place near Sarasota, where $40 cash and a note for $100 more could buy twenty-six acres more or less on Catfish Creek. It was three miles from the bay, not as close as we might have liked but as close as we could afford. There was an overgrown garden and an abandoned orange grove on the property – in other words nothing but work, and plenty of possibilities for the future.

Clarinda mentioned the obvious, that there was much to be done to make the property livable, and I suggested inviting Reuben to move over to help us. She expressed her concerns about his unarguably bad influence, but ultimately said okay.

Before leaving for our new home in the country, Clarinda said her goodbyes to Mrs. Abbe, her daughters and her grandkids, whom she visited often and to whom she had become attached. There were many hugs and a few tears, but Mrs. Abbe also took Clarinda aside for one whispered bit of advice.

"Before I knew who you were, I happened to be out in the front yard when you first rode into town on that old buckboard of yours. A Raggedy Ann you were, with that big gun on your lap. I was curious about you, of course. And I saw that man Jasper Braxton riding so proud down the street, and I heard what he said to you."

"I'm sure I've forgotten about that," Clarinda lied.

"Well, he said how pretty you were. But I do want to tell you, now I've gotten to know you and your new husband, as young as you both may be, that I really believe your Gawain is the much better man and the one you want to have along in life's journey. He's rough, but decent. And he'll do well."

"That's so nice of you to say, and I know he's the one for me," Clarinda gushed, as she ran out the door. But she could still feel the tingle Mr. Braxton with his blond hair and waxed mustache had left her with.

CHAPTER TWENTY-THREE
THE TRIAL

After all of my remembrances about my married life the reader may have forgotten about the assassins. Yet finally the trial of the Sarasota Vigilance Society came around. I expected to be the star witness so, of course, I attended.

It took a couple of days to pick a jury, so notorious was the crime. Two crimes, actually – the murder of Postmaster Abbe and, before that, the murder of Harrison "Tip" Riley. Willard was also charged with attempted murder for shooting Captain Duff, but his trial for that was to be held at a later date, if the guilty didn't get disposed of in the first rounds.

The Attorney General for the entire State of Florida came down from Tallahassee to assist with the prosecution. First they took up the killing of Tip Riley, and the star witness was one of the killers, Lewis Cato, the bootlegger and hardscrabble farmer from Phillippi Creek, who had decided to testify for the state. He described how the secret society worked, with all its special handshakes, rites, and oaths, and that

Alfred Bidwell, Jason Alford and Dr. Andrews were the "judges." (Jason Alford, by the way, was not in attendance. He had eluded capture and run off to Georgia.) There were twenty-two members of what was now described as the "Sarasota Assassination Society" by the reporters from the New York and Baltimore papers.

These three imperial "judges" had drawn up the list of those who were to die, and they assigned which of the violent young men were to carry out which murder. Cato further testified that there were five on the kill list that he knew about, but they had only gotten around to Tip Riley and Postmaster Abbe before they were all arrested.

Bidwell supplied Lewis Cato and Ed Bacon with a double-barrel shotgun and sent them to the road Riley was expected to take to town. In case Riley took a different route there were backup plans. Jason Alford and Dr. Hunter were sent to a foot-log over Phillippi Creek to lie in wait. Joe Anderson and Charley Willard were to go to the horse ford known as Brown's Crossing.

Cato went on to confess that he and Ed Bacon went as ordered to the road. "When Riley came both of us fired. Bacon used Bidwell's gun. I had a .22. We ran up. I cut Tip's throat, God help, me. The man had a damned tough hide! But I never did truly know why we had to kill the postmaster."

CATO'S BROTHER-IN-LAW, PREACHER LOWE'S STORY,
as told to the <u>New York Times</u>

I preach at Bee Ridge Friendship Baptist, and I know that Lewis Cato is a DAMN thug! He and his thug friends waylaid me in my own front yard up on Bee Ridge and whipped me within an inch of my life, and I'm an old man. They said they were delivering a sentence handed down by some DAMN "Society," but they were only being their own mean and sorry selves. I married Lewis's brother's widow Rebecca, and took in her boy and raised him like my own, but they still think that boy is a Cato, not a Lowe. And, Lord! Don't ever say anything bad about a Cato. I told that boy that, if he didn't stop hanging out with that drinking unreligious gang of them, the Lord would strike him dead unless I did it first. I said he could choose between them or decency, and if it was them he could forget about inheriting any of my property or his mother's. Mrs. Lowe's property is mine to do with, so that was included in my threat. Lewis Cato hated that, and he called me every name he could think of, which wasn't too many 'cause he ain't that smart.

That didn't work so he sic'd his dogs on me. Cato is a DOG! That's right. "For without the Gates of MY city are dogs, and sorcerers, and whoremongers, and murderers, and idolaters, and whosoever loveth and maketh a lie." That describes all of them and their wicked "society." But if you write any of this down I'll deny I said it. Family comes first for me.

William A. Bartholomew was called to testify. You will recall that when Tip Riley was murdered, Bartholomew served as the coroner. He testified that upon his arrival he viewed the body, still lying face down in the road. When Riley was turned over, it was apparent that his throat was cut from the ear to the windpipe. There were shot holes through this shirt and coat in the area his heart. The penetrations in the deceased's chest were probably big enough to put three fingers through.

After holding this inquest, Bartholomew had ruled that the death was by persons unknown. He authorized the burial, and there was no further investigation of the crime. Case closed. No one bothered to ask Bartholomew why he was so quick to close the case – especially since it was clear the man had been murdered.

During the testimony, the defendants were seated at two long tables, guarded by deputies at both ends. I caught Willard's eye and gave him a scowl. Willard winked back. He had shown up in court clean shaven except for that neat mustache and had dressed up nicely in navy blue suit and black necktie. You could hardly recognize him as the man I had hauled into jail not that long ago.

Willard passed a note over his shoulder to a man seated on the pew behind him, who stood up quietly and walked it over to me. He looked familiar, and might have been one of the teamsters I had crossed paths with at the Peace River. On the outside of the paper he had addressed me in pencil as "Det MacFarlane", and inside I read, "Does no soul care why I did this?"

I wrote back, "I do. Tell me why," and I passed it back. After studying it carefully, Charley looked my way. He raised his cupped hand to his mouth – like taking a drink. He grinned and gave me his laugh like a horse whinny. That got the attention of the judge, and the prisoner quickly straightened up. He gave his attention to the defense lawyers calling their first witness. And you never heard such lies!

Alfred Bidwell swore up and down that he had been to but one meeting of what he called a social organization formed for "political purposes" to promote "a better feeling in that neighborhood among neighbors." He missed any subsequent meetings because he fell ill. "I stayed in bed for four weeks. I never heard a word," he claimed, "about killing anyone, or any by-laws."

What was most remarkable to me was that a number of prominent citizens highly placed in the legal community of Buffalo, Bidwell's last hometown, where a statue had been erected in honor of his brother the Civil War hero, submitted affidavits attesting to Alfred Bidwell's spotless character and reputation throughout the State of New York. One noted, as an aside, that prior to Alfred's moving to Florida, "it was a general understanding that he had divorced his wife, or, "at least, they separated."

That bunch of horse-pucky was followed up by Dr. Leonard Andrews. Feigning sickness, he was helped to the stand by his defense lawyers, a team that included top attorneys from Tampa and Jacksonville. Who, one must ask, was paying their bills? The doctor testified that in May of 1884, Jason Alford had approached him and said, "We're going to organize a 'social club' to stop 'slander' in our community and use the 'influence of good men to do away with it, and make peace and harmony among the citizens.'" Another Bee Ridge neighbor, "one of the Redd boys," was already in the club according to Andrews. "He said it was in the best interests of the citizens and peace and harmony, and that decided me because he was a deacon in my church."

Dr. Andrews admitted that he had attended a meeting of the Assassination Society – though he didn't call it that - where there was talk of Tip Riley getting "strapped" because the court had turned him loose on the adultery charge. But there had been no mention of any murders.

Dr. Andrews also came prepared with affidavits. Half a dozen citizens from Cass County, Iowa, from whence he had come, had been visited by lawyers and provided sworn statements that Dr. Leonard Andrews was held in the highest regard in that state and had made many meritorious contributions to their community.

After all that bull, the prosecution of Charley Willard, Ed Bacon, and the other defendants for the murder of Postmaster Abbe was surprisingly short. Charles Morehouse, who had witnessed Abbe being killed, gave a graphic account of the events of that morning, including seeing Willard argue on the beach with Mr. Abbe, seeing Willard rise from the bushes and shoot Mr. Abbe, and being told by Willard to run away. The postmaster's poor widow testified tearfully about hearing the shot and rushing out of the house, and seeing her husband's blood in the sand. She would be forever furious that his body had been stolen away.

Sheriff Watson testified concerning his arrival on the scene, his investigation of the crime, and the arrest of Joe Anderson. And the later arrests of the remaining conspirators based upon the information that I had supplied. He mentioned me by my name, Deputy Gawain Wallace MacFarlane, and also acknowledged that I had arrested Charley Willard myself, after other men had given up the chase.

To my great disappointment, however, I was not called to the stand, though I was more than ready to tell my story on the record. Nevertheless, I don't suppose it would have been necessary because neither Charlie Willard nor Ed Bacon testified or put on a single witness. After all, what was there to say?

The judge stood up, whacked his gavel and loudly proclaimed, "The jury's out!"

Well, they weren't out long, less than two hours.

Charley Willard and Joe Anderson were found guilty of murder in the first degree for shooting Mr. Abbe. The jury begged the mercy of the court. That disgusted me since I thought they should pay with their lives, yet the Court spared them from the gallows and gave them both life in the penitentiary at hard labor.

Dr. Hunter was let off, even though Willard had indicated to me that he was probably one of those who dragged Abbe's body down to the beach. Charley, however, had not been positive about that because he said he had been extremely drunk at the time, as Dr. Hunter had also been.

Most satisfying to me was that Bidwell and Dr. Andrews were both found guilty of being "accessories before the fact" in the postmaster's ambush. Ed Bacon was found not guilty of murdering Mr. Abbe, which was wrong, but he got convicted for the murder of Tip Riley. And there was no recommendation of mercy for any of them! This was the first time in Manatee County history that a jury had not requested that a guilty murderer be permitted to live in prison, given another chance as it were.

The three of them, Bacon, Bidwell and Andrews, were sentenced to hang. They all appealed.

CHAPTER TWENTY-FOUR

MY TOWN

After the trial was over the newspapers picked up the story of my tenacious pursuit of the murderer, Charley Willard, focusing on my persistence when others had quit and returned to the safety of their homes. Though I couldn't see how these stories would help me get along with my neighbors, they nevertheless did make me well-known as an up-and-coming young local man. Out in the countryside, at our new home, the wives and mothers in both directions had something to talk about with Clarinda, and she began making friends. This helped her put up with the appearance of Reuben, whom I lodged in the corn crib of our fallen-down barn that as yet had no livestock in residence. He had the place cleared of rats and snakes in no time.

But the news about the Assassination Society did not end with the article about my heroism. Alfred Bidwell's death sentence was commuted to life at hard labor. He had received this favor from the governor. People in town said that Jasper Braxton, for reasons of his own, had paid a lot of people to get that pardon for the mastermind of the "Society" of killers.

Dr. Leonard Andrews and Ed Bacon apparently couldn't count on Jasper Braxton's benevolent intervention. They grabbed a guard's shotgun and escaped from the Pine Level jail. Hearing that, I was sure to keep my own gun handed, loaded and ready.

As a matter of fact, I was out buying cartridges and other supplies for my new place when I ran into Creed Driggers buying his own boxes of shotgun shells and .38's at the dry goods store.

"You're a ways from home," I said amicably.

Driggers scowled at me, trying to remember where he had seen me, and when it came to him his expression didn't soften. "You're that deputy who was sneaking around my place," he said.

"I wasn't sneaking," I said, offended. "I was on your side."

"Well, fuck you very much," Driggers told me. "Those boys burned me out."

"Wait, somebody burned you out? You mean your house?"

"Whole damn place up in smoke. Nearly killed my wife. But they didn't," he said, settling up his bill at the counter and making to leave. "We may be sleeping in a goddam tent, but we ain't going nowhere. So you still got me to deal with!"

"Hey, I didn't do it!" I protested.

Driggers turned to confront me. "What happened to that forged quitclaim deed you said you found?"

"I gave it to the sheriff for evidence and haven't seen it since."

"God damn! You lyin' sonofabitch! That deed's down in the courthouse. I'd shoot you right here if I wasn't in town! Just stay out of my way! And keep off my property!"

I was stung by the insult but so caught off guard by its ferocity that I stood there like a fool with my mouth agape while Driggers yanked open the door and stomped through it.

"I ain't beat and I ain't broke," I heard Driggers shout. "I'll pick the daisies off your fucking graves!" The door slammed behind him.

"That's an angry individual," the storekeeper commented.

Which got me to wondering. I confided my concerns to Captain Duff.

 The Captain knew his way around real estate trades, and he explained to me that the Great State Development Company and Jasper Braxton were the same thing, and they were all in bed with the Florida Mortgage and Investment Company. He said it was common knowledge that these men, men like Braxton, had set their sights on running all the settlers off the land and building empires of their own to populate with immigrants from "up North." The Captain acknowledged that population growth would benefit his lumberyard, since empires meant new construction, but then again, the title to his own acreage went back to squatters, and maybe that could be questioned by someone.

Notwithstanding these concerns, he asked me if I'd like a job, which could be selling lumber, or it could be delivering it. Lumber was a good business to be in, he said.

"I do appreciate the offer, Captain Duff, but I think I'd better see if I can make a go of farming."

"Well, you know you've got a wife to look after now, and there may be kids on the way. A steady paycheck is a good thing to have."

"Yessir, I'll keep that in mind," I assured him, because it was the truth. "But right now, I think I'd better tell the sheriff about Mister Braxton." I wasn't prepared for the Captain's reply.

"I expect Sandy knows all about that," he said. "He knows about that and more."

Now I wanted to know all about that "and more," too. But I would learn it from the source. "Where exactly does this Jasper Braxton hang his hat?" I asked.

The Captain gave me directions, and I followed them for an hour to the Braxton ranch. It was a nice spread situated in a bend of the Braden River, right before where it flows into the Manatee. There was a gate on the road, and burned into the wooden plank were the words Dove's Rest. The gate was open, and I rode in at least a quarter of a mile before I saw the house, which was long and flat and built of pine logs. It wasn't a rustic cabin though, but a fancy place with stables and barns around it. A woman, mounted on a black horse which I reckoned to be about a hand taller at the withers than my own Whistler, rode out of a corral to see who I was. I told her I was looking for Jasper Braxton.

"What for?" she asked, studying my face and my striking chin full of soft whiskers.

I studied her right back. A nice looking lady with a blue checkered shirt and brown hair tied back with a red bandana, a few years older than me. "He asked me to see him about a job," I told her.

"Then he's out on the range, about a mile south." She pointed with her crop. And smiled at me.

"'Preciate it," I said and rode off in that direction.

I found Braxton overseeing a group of cowboys branding calves. They had a fire of pine knots going, and were wrestling the calves onto the ground one-by-one and burning on their brand, DR in a circle.

Braxton rode over and sidled up beside me. "Come to take me up on my offer?" he asked.

"I'm here to find out what the job is," I said.

"Let's go over a sit by those trees. Braxton trotted his horse to a large oak shading the edge of the field and dismounted. He let the reins drop onto the ground and squatted in the grass, where I joined him.

"What kind of name is Gawain?" Braxton asked me, sociably enough.

"I don't know exactly what it means, but it's supposed to be Scottish. I'm told my family came from Scotland though I can't tell you much about it."

"You know, there's supposed to be a whole colony of Scottish people coming in here soon," he said. "Any kin to you?"

"Not that I know of. I never heard about any colony either."

"Well, just on account of your name, Gawain Wallace MacFarlane, they might find you a useful person to know." He said each of my names very carefully. I was surprised that he knew them, but I didn't ask him how. "Of course," Braxton continued, "with a law enforcement background there's other ways I could maybe use you, too."

I just nodded.

"I'm on the lookout for a man who can lead other men, who can get them to go where he tells 'em to go and do what he tells 'em to do, and who's smart enough to keep his mouth shut."

"What's the pay?" I asked.

"Could be as much as three dollars a day, or even more depending on performance."

I plucked a piece of grass to suck on, but I was impressed. That sure was a lot of money. "I've got to ask you some questions," I said.

"Shoot 'em out there," Braxton told me.

"It seems to me like you and William Bartholomew and that whole assassination group was tied in together some way."

"We weren't tied up in any way that matters, Mister Lawman, but I know what makes these people tick."

"What is that?'

"Community service for some, I'd say. For others it's a chance to be mean as a snake and get away with it. But for Alfred Bidwell, it was just about money, and prestige."

"You're speaking of them like they're gone. They ain't gone," I said.

He laughed. "To me they are," he said. He glanced around to be sure no one else was in earshot. "They did everything Bidwell told them to do," he continued, "and he did everything I paid him to do. Which was to clear this vicinity of some troublesome competitors and squatters. Bidwell would have had a better future if he hadn't been caught. He could have been a big shot, which is all he ever wanted to be."

"A big shot like you?"

Braxton also thought that was funny. "Not that big," he said. "But I would have made a place for him in the company."

"The Florida Mortgage and Investment Company? Limited?" I asked.

"That's what I'm talking about. You're smart. Take it from me, they're coming. And sooner than you think. Get on board with me."

"Everybody that I know who works for you is going to jail."

"Maybe so. Or maybe not. But not for very long."

"They'll get the rope."

"Doubt that."

I felt more surprise than I showed. After a pause, I asked, "What did they kill poor Tip Riley for?"

"Moral infractions, I suppose. He also sat on land that they wanted. Maybe I wanted it, too. Waylaying ol' Riley sure did give them a taste for killing, didn't it? I'm only answering these questions Gawain because I think you can understand the world we're in and the way it is going to be. Not all men are good."

"There's a lot of different ways of deciding who's good, seems to me. Bidwell and Dr. Andrews, both of 'em, had people back home, wherever they came from, saying how 'good' they was."

"Well, Gawain. The more respected you are, the better quality witnesses will lie for you."

I chewed that over. "I think Mister Abbe was a good man. Everybody said so. Why'd they have to kill him?"

"He stood in the way of development, I guess. I'll blame it on Bidwell. And they found some dumb cracker named Charley Willard to do their killing for them."

"I'm as much of a dumb cracker as he is."

"I wouldn't call you dumb, Gawain. I think you're smart enough or I wouldn't be offering you a job."

"I'm smart enough to wonder who paid for those lawyers, and how Ed Bacon and Dr. Andrews managed their escape from jail after being sentenced to hang."

"Those are damn good questions, and as close as you are to the sheriff, maybe you can find out the answers. But, as to Ed Bacon and Dr. Andrews, I'd say our community is better off since they left it."

"People think they got down to Punta Gorda and hired a boat for Cuba. Or else, one might have killed the other and buried him in the woods."

Braxton shook his head. "My guess is those two misguided men, though one is a medical doctor and one is just a shit-kicking redneck, are quite valuable to each other and will stick together as they make their murderous way through Florida. But I don't believe they'd go to Cuba. What would they do in Cuba? Their families are here in Florida. I expect they'll just lay low for a while out there in the wild, wild woods, and one day rise back to the surface."

"And do what for money?"

"There's always a way for a self-righteous man and a ruthless sidekick to make a living. They can always start a church." Braxton laughed. "Somehow they'll get by, I'm sure."

I stood up and dusted off my pants. "I appreciate the offer, Mister Braxton, and I can't deny it's good money," I said, "but I just got married and I think I'd like a safer way of life for a while. Also . . ." I added, "I'm coming to be of the opinion that what we need around here is more justice for the little man."

"Do you think you'll long stick with that point of view?" he asked.

"Let's just say the jury's out."

Braxton took his time getting up. "Suit yourself, Gawain," he said, straightening his shoulders. "I'll be around. And maybe we can do something together with those Scotsmen when they arrive."

"Maybe so," I told him. Watching each other like hawks, we parted ways.

Maybe so, I thought to himself, but I doubt it. I was satisfied just to get out of his company still alive.

As I was riding away from this interview on Whistler, I passed the corral where Braxton's wife was working a stallion, and I blew her a kiss. Probably I did it to show my disdain for her husband. But that kiss caught her eye.

God should punish me for doing that since I had just gotten married to Clarinda. It was wrong.

JASPER BRAXTON'S STORY

Maybe I shouldn't have been so forthright with Gawain MacFarlane, but I sensed some of the same hunger in him that I had always had. For glory? Maybe just success. Or beating all the odds. Anyway, the gavel of justice had come down on the whole Assassination Society, and I was as glad as anyone to see them go. Let's call it an experiment gone bad. As it turned out, they also were bad for the reputation of Southwest Florida and, more importantly, bad for promoting investment in real estate projects. Like the 60,000 acres the Florida Mortgage and Investment Company had selected me to clear of interlopers. The future was coming, boys, like it or not!

None of those Vigilante fools could tie me to anything, or would want to. I was their ticket to freedom. And Bartholomew is still on the payroll.

Hidden under all those miles of sawgrass and palmetto jungle, Florida has incredibly rich soil ideal for raising orange trees, and grapefruit, and pineapples, and just about any fruit or vegetable you can name. And the land can be had for pennies. For pennies! All you have to do is take it. The only thing that does cost some money is paying surveyors and bribing judges.

Who are you going to find to clear all that jungle and make it into farms? That's what my backers asked. The answer is as obvious as the nose on your face. We sell it in little bits and pieces to all the Yankees from Maine to Illinois *who want a fresh start, a chance to make a buck, a way to stay warm in the winter and who know how to work for their living. Don't worry. They will civilize the jungle. And if the new landowners need extra labor, why the shiftless squatters will work for next to nothing. Or you can import blacks aplenty from Georgia and Alabama. They are so happy to get off the cotton plantations that you hardly have to pay them anything at all.*

Lo and behold, investors by the dozen have appeared. Here comes the Florida Mortgage and Investment Company from Scotland. They have a big plan. But they aren't the only ones. I'm sitting on the biggest land grab in history, and I offer my services as local agent to enterprises far and wide.

A man like Charles Abbe posed a different problem. He was a U.S. Commissioner, a Republican holdover who didn't have to listen to the local politicians I can easily buy. He heard disputes involving federal lands, and homestead rights, and patents on new orange strains, matters of that sort. And damned if he didn't start advising squatters, when they came before him, about how they could survey their property and prove up their boundaries and establish how long they had farmed their little plots, and actually get legal title.

Having a bunch of cracker rednecks with their broods of children and stashes of firearms littering up our scrub and prairie lands can really mess up the attractiveness of real estate to potential buyers, you can believe that. So, they had to go, and the fools like Abbe had to go with them.

Just as a wise politician in Boston once told me, the gift of the mastermind is to remain behind the scenes. I have found that if you are quiet about it, there is literally no end to the schemes, all legal, that you can bring to fruition in Florida, this magnificent place.

When I got to the Sheriff's Office no one was there. This wasn't unusual in our small town. Since I had the advantage of privacy and I decided hurriedly to see what was in the sheriff's old safe. The combination was my own birthday, which had always made me feel that I had a special bond with Sheriff Watson.

But there was nothing in the safe but a packet of greenbacks. The payroll of the Sheriff's office, I assumed. But where was the Driggers quitclaim? Not there.

I rushed home to my Catfish Creek property to relate all of this to Clarinda. I went through all the intrigue, the conspiracies, the money I was being offered.

And she advised me to keep my nose out of other people's business. Settle in and get some work done on the property. Look after our family's welfare.

I didn't like her advice, but I took it. I applied myself to getting us a mule, a plow, and other items that we needed, but could barely afford. I slowly got our "holdings" productive. One item on her wishlist was a guitar. Clarinda had let on that she liked the sound of that particular instrument, and maybe a little picking would provide some extra evening entertainment. It wasn't long before I got it for her.

Reuben lent me a magazine containing a tale by a writer named Jack London called "An Old Soldier's Story," which I enjoyed. In an introduction the author said he had made it his vow to learn three new words a day. That impressed me since I also had scant education but wanted to write about my adventures, and I bought a dictionary for our house. With Clarinda's picture book of birds, a songbook and a Bible, now we had ourselves a little library. And I started learning those three new words.

Our life was happy, but while buying more supplies at a store on Phillippi Creek, I learned that Jasper Braxton had declared for Circuit Judge. He was running against an incumbent Republican, and he had a good chance of winning, though people said he was a rich asshole.

What was really surprising was that Sandy Watson was supporting him. And, the sheriff was retiring!

There was a lot of politics all happening at the same time. In addition to Sandy Watson stepping down, the State Legislature was carving off Desoto County out of Manatee, and taking Pine Level with it. There was a vote to determine a new county seat for what was left of the county, and Bradentown won the right to absorb Manatee City and the courthouse. Of course, it didn't take many voters to make a decision like that, since you had to be white, a landowner, a man, and have no black marks on your record in order to vote. And pay a poll tax. That eliminated nine-and-a-half-tenths of the population.

But, on a brighter note, I learned that Mrs. Alfred Bidwell, the assassin's wife, had been forced by economic constraints to put her house in Sarasota up for sale, since her husband was disgraced and now in prison, having barely avoided the gallows by commutation. And even better, Charlotte Abbe was appointed Postmaster for Sarasota.

One day Clarinda came back from a trip to town with the "news" that a whole colony of families from Scotland were arriving to settle in Sarasota. "They know we have a paradise here, compared to where they come from," which was how the story was being presented to our small populace.

"That's amazing!" And I did think so. There's a lot I wanted to know about Scotland. Not only did my family come from there, but the Scots could probably explain what some of the words in those Robert Burns poems actually meant.

Marriage suited me, but on a trip to Manatee City to share my new life with Sheriff Watson, I happened to pass the first girl I'd ever kissed and who kissed me back, red-headed Loralie. She beckoned me over and commented favorably about my "fame" as a lawman. She was just as pretty as I remembered her, and I had to stop myself from telling her so. "But I got to go now," I concluded, and snapped Whistler's reins. "See you around," she called after me. I had sworn to myself that I would be always be true to Clarinda. And I believed that, until one day I wasn't.

My life and my place in the community kept evolving. In conversations with Mrs. Abbe, she told me that since Sarasota was starting to boom, it might soon incorporate. And as a growing town, it needed a constable to keep order. She urged me to apply for the job.

I did so immediately. Now that I was a landowning citizen, I had a stake, and I knew there were plenty of things that needed to be straightened out. That forged quitclaim deed on Creed Driggers' property, for instance, and the nightriders burning down settlers' cabins all over the county. And somebody had to be on the lookout for those murderous escapees, Dr. Andrews and Ed Bacon, and lots of other criminals on the loose. Southwest Florida was full of them. There was no place for any of that in my town.

Clarinda may have given me good advice about staying clear of politics, but for a sharp old fellow like Captain Duff that wasn't an option. Ever since he had arrived in Florida, he had quickly seen that everything was political. The crowd in control kept changing, as more and more money rolled in, as the railroads laid more tracks, as more tourists discovered the beaches and more developers built hotels, but there was always a "crowd" in control.

Captain Duff's kinsman, Sandy Watson, his brother-in-arms, might have gone off the rails, but that was his business. "Maybe I'll run for Sheriff," Duff said to his wife, who just rolled her eyes.

But he was serious. In time, the struggle to contain the land thieves and chart the future of Florida would come to dominate the Captain's last years. And for me, who just wanted to be left alone to build my own life, I would be drawn in as well. And my destiny was to be a lawman.

I'll tell about that in due course.

I, nor anyone else, save Jasper Braxton, truly saw what was coming.

THE END